The next kiss was long and slow. She tasted like wine and smoke, and as she pushed me down on my back on the couch, I knew I had been starving to death for this without even knowing it.

Compared to what Susan did to me that night, what Angel and me had done had just been little girl tea parties. Angel was a girl, but Susan was a woman — a woman who knew exactly what she was doing.

Before I knew it, I was out of my dress and on the floor, and she was on top of me with her thigh between my legs. We were moving, moving, moving until I thought I'd go crazy, and then the whole room was shaking like an earthquake. But the earthquake was coming from me.

Phases of the Moon

Julia Watts

THE NAIAD PRESS, INC.
1997

Printed in the United States of America on acid-free paper
First Edition

Editor: Lila Empson
Cover designer: Bonnie Liss (Phoenix Graphics)
Typesetter: Sandi Stancil

Library of Congress Cataloging-in-Publication Data

Watts, Julia, 1969–
Phases of the moon / by Julia Watts.
p. cm.
ISBN 1-56280-176-7 (pbk.)
I. Title.
PS3573.A868P48 1997
813′.54—dc21 97-10809
CIP

Acknowledgments

Special thanks to the Kentucky Foundation for Women for deeming my work worthy of financial assistance; to expert editor Lila Empson, who has the daunting job of making sure that all my Appalachian speech is spelled correctly; and to Barbara Grier and the tirelessly working women of Naiad Press. Even though *Phases of the Moon* is a work of fiction, factual information on the world of country and rockabilly music gave me the knowledge to create realistic fictional characters and settings. For this information, Mary Bufwack and Robert Oermann's *Finding Her Voice: The Saga of Women in Country Music* was indispensable. Also, the interview with Lynn Peril in V. Vale and Andrea Juno's *Incredibly Strange Music* made it possible for me to actually get my hands on some hard-to-find recordings by women in rockabilly music.

As always, I must express my undying gratitude to Carol Guthrie, Don Windham, and Ian Windham for putting up with my neurotic writer's personality on a daily basis and to my mom and dad, who are as good at proofreading as they are at parenting. And finally, I'd like to acknowledge the friends who have complimented my work, attended my readings, or given me a place to crash when I was reading in their city. They are (in alphabetical order) Allison, Dwane, Helen, Jason, Jim, Keri, Melissa, Patrick, Stephanie, and Tab.

About the Author

A native of Southeastern Kentucky, Julia Watts is a part-time teacher, a part-time nanny, and a "rest-of-the-time" writer. This year, she was able to devote more time than usual to her writing, thanks to a generous grant from the Kentucky Foundation for Women. She is the author of one previous novel, *Wildwood Flowers,* also published by Naiad Press.

Chapter 1

Listen. If you're gonna write my life story like you say you want to, I don't want you to spend a lot of time talking about me being born in a two-room house and growing up poor and all that. People don't want to read about that stuff; it's depressing. And besides, does it really matter how I got here? It's like when you get the educated people and the religious people arguing about evolution and creation. I say, what does it matter how we got here? It seems like the real thing to worry about is how we're all gonna get along now that we are here.

So we'll just take it as a given that I got born and grew some. No need to waste time talking about that. As far as I'm concerned, there's only two things worth talking about anyway, and that's music and love. And my story starts with music.

I was twelve years old when my brothers Roy and Vaughn ordered them each a Silvertone guitar from the Sears and Roebuck catalog. Where they got the money I still don't know — gambling, maybe, or stealing somebody's calf and selling it. I love my big brothers to death, but I wouldn't put anything past them.

But the day those guitars came, that was some big excitement. Argon, Kentucky, where we lived, was just a wide place in the road. There was the mines and a little store with a built-in post office, and that was it. So getting a package in the mail was always exciting, even if it was just something ordinary like new shoes for school.

But those Silvertone guitars were the most beautiful things I had ever seen. So new and shiny — I remember the sunlight gleaming off Vaughn's as he lifted it out of its case on the porch. And the wood was so smooth. As I ran my hand over that guitar's curves, I tingled with pleasure I didn't even understand.

"Don't touch it, Sissy," Vaughn warned. "I don't want your ol' fingerprints all over it."

Mama came out on the porch about that time, looking worried like she always did. "Boys," she said, wrapping her arms around her chest like it was cold even though it was summertime, "where'd you get the money to buy them guitars?"

"Mama," Roy said, grinning like a salesman, "me

and Vaughn has decided to take up the Lord's music."

It wasn't a real answer, and I'm sure Mama knew it, but you didn't ask questions when the name of the Lord came up, so she clamped her lips together real tight, then turned to me and said, "Glenda, come on in and help me with the dinner dishes."

I looked back at the guitars, not wanting to leave them, but did as Mama told me. Vaughn and Roy stayed on the porch, laughing.

As it turned out, though, Roy was right. They did end up playing the Lord's music. Every night after supper, they'd sit out on the porch with their guitars, sneaking sips from a flask of whiskey and trying to pick out tunes. I'd rush through doing the dishes, not even bothering to dry them good, so I could go out there and be near that music.

It wasn't even good music, really. All you could say for Roy was that he could pick out a tune good enough that you could recognize it, and you couldn't even say that much for Vaughn. The more Vaughn drank from that flask, the worse he played. But still, I had to be near those guitars. Every note that rang out of them, even the wrong notes, was calling to me. I was like one of those cobras that comes out of a basket, charmed by music, you see on those nature programs.

And so every night I'd sit there, getting eaten alive by mosquitoes, not knowing anything except that I had to be there. And one night after dark, when the lightning bugs were flashing on and off real pretty and I knew that Mama would be coming out soon in her nightgown to tell me to go to bed, that night was when I first opened up my mouth to sing.

It just happened; I didn't know I was gonna do it till I'd already done it. Roy was picking out "In the Sweet By and By" so it sounded pretty good, and suddenly this voice I had never heard before was rolling out of me. Oh, I had sung a little before, moved my lips along with hymns in church. But this was different. This was the first time I really opened my mouth up, and my voice was clear and big — bigger than me. It rang out through the hollow and up to the mountains, and suddenly I felt like one of those lightning bugs, like there was a fire that was lighting me up from the inside.

"Well, I'll be goddamned, Sissy," Roy said when we had finished. "You can sing."

Vaughn was looking at me like he didn't even know who I was. "That was real good," he said.

I laughed like a crazy person because I had just found something wonderful that up until that minute I didn't even know I had.

Mama came out on the porch in her nightgown, but instead of telling me to go to bed, she said, "Glenda Fay, was that you I heard singin' just now?"

"Yes'm."

"Well, then," she said, real matter of fact, "I reckon singin's your God gift."

Roy and Vaughn soon figured out a way to put my "God gift" to use. The next night when we were out on the porch, Roy took a swig of whiskey and said, "Listen, Sissy, me and Vaughn's been talkin' about how good you sing, and we was thinkin' maybe we could put us together a group."

"A group?"

"Yeah," Vaughn said, "you know, a singin' group. You could be the girl singer, and Roy could play the guitar, and I could kindly strum along and try not to get my fingers caught in the strings."

"We could play in churches," Roy added.

"In churches?" I laughed. "Neither of you'uns has darkened the door of a church since your voices changed. How come you wanna start gettin' religion now?"

Roy grinned real sly. "It ain't about religion, sissy. It's about money. These little ol' churches — you go play music in 'em, and you get to pass around a bucket for donations. Love offerings, they call 'em. Our buddy Bobby says he can take us around in his daddy's Ford if he can get a cut of the money."

"But goin' around to churches and singin' just so you can take people's money don't seem right."

"Oh, don't get all prissy on us, Glenda," Vaughn said. "With the voice you've got, the people'd be gettin' their money's worth."

"And besides," Roy added, "you want to sing, don't you?"

I did. More than anything. And that was how the Singing Mooney Family was born.

Chapter 2

We went to a bunch of churches that summer. Roy and Vaughn would put on the good shirts and pants they usually only wore to funerals, and I'd wear my powder-blue, puffed-sleeve dress that Mama made me and tie my hair back with a matching blue ribbon. Roy said it was real important that I look cute because a cute little girl singing the Lord's music would make people dig deep into their pockets quicker than anything.

After we'd get dressed up, we'd pile into Bobby's car, and Bobby and Roy and Vaughn would pass a bottle of whiskey around while we twisted and turned down the country roads that would take us to the church where we were singing.

The places we sang at were all little churches with big names, like The Sacred Holy Sign Following Church of God in Jesus' Blessed Name. They usually wouldn't have more than six pews, and there'd always be a gourd dipper hanging on the wall next to a bucket of drinking water. The church would be packed full of country people, women in their best print dresses and men in their clean overalls. You could always count on a good crowd. Back in the sticks, there wasn't much to do for entertainment but go to church.

And lord, did I keep those people entertained! Honey, sometimes I'd get so carried away singing that poor ol' Vaughn would stop even trying to keep up with me and just end up slapping his guitar in time like a drum. I had never thought of myself as a religious person before, but when I got up in front of a crowd of people singing, it was like I was possessed by some power greater than me. And at the time, I just kind of assumed it was the power of Jesus.

That power allowed me to whip those church crowds into a frenzy. The women, particularly. When I sang, it was like I released some feeling in them they had kept pent up when they were cooking and washing clothes and taking care of babies. They'd jump up and down and clap their hands and dance themselves into a frenzy even though they were supposed to believe that dancing was sinful. For that five or ten minutes I was singing, they were free.

One night when we were playing "In the Sweet By and By," I kept singing faster and faster, and then before I knew it I was running up and down the aisle singing "I want somebody to testify, won't somebody testify" over and over. And then this woman stood up. She was one of those real thin, stringy-haired women, but her face was glowing like a lit-up jack-o'-lantern. And when she started talking, it wasn't in English or in any language I've heard before or since. Sounds just kept spilling out of her mouth: "Abalala shabala mallingo." I just looked at her, almost scared, not knowing what to do, when this real old woman on the other side of the room stood up and said, "She says the Holy Spirit has done took over this room tonight. She says that the Holy Spirit liveth in the music, and God will use the music to take us where he sees fit."

The preacher shouted "praise God," and there were lots of other *praise God*s and *praise Jesus*es and *amen*s. I didn't know what to do to follow an act of God, so I just broke back into "In the Sweet By and By," and before I knew it, everybody was on their feet and clapping. Roy decided this was a good opportunity to pass the donation bucket around, and by the time it got back to us, it was brimming with dollar bills.

When we finally made it back to the car — we had to keep stopping for people to hug us and say "God bless you" — Bobby, who never went inside the churches, grabbed the bucket and said, "Good god-a-mighty, there must be a hunnert dollars in here!"

"Oh, you should've seen Sissy up there," Vaughn said. "She put on a helluva show."

"Yeah, what got into you anyway, Sissy?" Roy

turned around in the front seat to eye me. He had the whiskey bottle in one hand and a cigarette in the other. "And don't tell me it was no Holy Spirit neither."

"I don't know," I said. "I was just singin', I reckon." To tell the truth, I did think the spirit of the Lord had descended upon me, but there was no way I was gonna say that to my brothers. It was none of their damn business anyway.

Every Sunday and Wednesday night that summer we were off somewhere singing. Every other night, my brothers were out spending the money we made on God knows what. Even though I did most of the work, I didn't actually get my hands on much of the proceeds from our "love offerings." Roy and Vaughn and Bobby figured they needed the money worse than I did because they were older, and besides, I was a girl. I should've minded, but I didn't. At the time, getting to sing in front of an appreciative audience was payment enough. Besides, I told myself that unlike Roy and Vaughn and Bobby, my motives were pure.

The first part of that summer is a blur of memories of riding to churches and getting out of the car and hoping the church people couldn't smell the whiskey and cigarettes on my brothers' breath. But the middle of that June is as clear in my memory as what I had for breakfast this morning. It was in the middle of June when Angel came to Argon, and if I close my eyes right this second, I can still see every freckle on her face.

I was sitting on the porch with Mama, shucking corn. Mama worked silently, like she always did, with great concentration. I was off in a daydream, not paying any attention to what I was doing and leaving too many little stringy things on the corn.

And before I knew what was happening, Mama was nudging me and saying, "Well, goodness gracious, child. Can't you at least say hello?"

I looked up, and standing before me was a hard-eyed little man in a dark suit and the most beautiful girl I had ever seen.

It was like she had stepped out of my daydream. Here I had been all summer, running around with nasty old boys or else helping Mama with chores, which was no fun because I hated housework and because all Mama ever talked about was people who were sick or dead. But now there was this girl, who looked to be my own age. This girl, who had long, naturally curly red hair like I had always wanted and a faceful of freckles that made her look friendly somehow.

Her pink lips curled up in a little smile. "Cat got your tongue?"

The man laughed. "Miss Glenda, I'm Brother Daniel Dixon, and this here's my daughter Angel. People round here been tellin' me you're the star member of the Singin' Mooney Family."

If the cat hadn't got my tongue, Angel sure had. Angel. It was the perfect name for her. Mama draped her arm around me and said, "She sings real good."

"That's what I been hearin'," Brother Dixon boomed. "Well, I've come here from plumb over in Harlan. A feller over there told me you'uns has been without a Baptist preacher for some time, and I got to thinkin' about that, and well, I reckon you could say the Lord spoke to me. And the long and short of it is, I've come to do the Lord's work here in Argon." He looked down at Angel, who hadn't taken her ice-blue eyes off me for a second. "Course, my little Angel, she don't know nobody 'round here, and I was thinkin' it might be good if she had a nice Christian girl to show her the sights."

I looked at Angel and felt my face heating up like I was coming down with a fever. Mama nudged me. "Well, there ain't much to show," I mumbled, "But I reckon I'll see what I can do." Angel grinned like up till then she hadn't been sure if I liked her or not.

Brother Dixon pressed two nickels into my hand. "Well, I'll tell you what, Miss Glenda," he said, "You'uns can start by goin' down to the store and havin' a Co-Cola on me."

"What do you say, Glenda?" Mama said.

"Thank you, Brother Dixon."

"The only way I want you to thank me, Miss Glenda, is by bein' down at the Argon Missionary Baptist Church this Sunday and lettin' me hear your purty voice."

Angel grabbed my hand and led me down the road from our house. As we walked away, I heard Mama say to Brother Dixon, "I don't know what's wrong with that girl today. Most times I can't get her to hush."

I didn't care if Mama thought I was acting funny. All I cared about was my hand being in Angel's as she led me down the dirt road in front of the house. And even as we came to the store, I wanted her to keep walking, to keep leading me, to keep my hand in hers. She could have walked me plumb out of

Kentucky and into Tennessee. She could have walked me and walked me, and if the world was flat like people used to think it was, she could have walked me right over the edge into space, just so long as I could have held on to that soft little hand.

Chapter 3

You couldn't have pulled Angel and me apart with a crowbar. And at first, that was just fine by everybody. Mama liked having another girl around the house, since she hadn't had much luck having baby girls, except for me. Roy and Vaughn told Angel to stick around for a couple of years, and they'd be fighting to court her. Brother and Mrs. Dixon were tickled that their daughter had found a new friend so fast. Even my daddy, who didn't pay much attention to us kids most of the time, would grin a little when he saw Angel and say, "How ya doin', Red?"

And me, I couldn't have been happier. I had my music, and I had Angel. She'd go with us sometimes when we'd sing, and I'd sit on her lap in the backseat of Bobby's car so we could all fit in. She would wrap her arms around my waist so I wouldn't get jerked around too much, and I would lean back against her and hide my face in her sweet-smelling hair until it felt like I was looking at the world through an orange waterfall.

I always sang my best when Angel would come with us. I'd look out and see her in the front pew smiling at me, and it was like my whole body turned into a song. The love of God was the only kind of love I had ever really heard anybody talk about, so I just kind of assumed that while I was up there singing and looking at Angel, the love of God was what I was feeling. But what was I feeling in the car when I sat on Angel's lap and buried my face in her hair? All I knew about that feeling was that it felt good.

Angel felt it, too. Once when I was spending the night at her house and we were lying in her bed under her pink chenille peacock bedspread, she said, "Do you ever go to the show, Glenda?"

"I've been to the show a few times, when we was visitin' Mama's people over in Morgan. Mama used to go to the show all the time before she met Daddy. She named me after a movie actress, you know."

Angel was real quiet for a minute, long enough to let me figure out that all she had wanted was a simple yes or no answer. Then she said, "You know how men and women kiss in the movies — when they kinda hug each other and close their eyes and move their mouths together real slow? Like Tarzan and Jane do?"

"Uh-huh."

"Well, sometimes I feel like doin' that with you."

I thought about it for a minute. "Well, you reckon we could?"

Angel laughed. "We got mouths, don't we?"

"Well, yeah, I was just wonderin' . . . you know, if it would be wrong."

"I sure don't see nothin' wrong with it. I mean, you and me both love Jesus, and we love each other in the spirit of true friendship, don't we?"

"Uh-huh."

"Well then, I don't see what'd be wrong with it. It don't seem half as bad to me as your brothers gettin' knee-walkin' drunk on the way to church."

We giggled for a few minutes the way only twelve-year-old girls can. Then we both got real quiet, and Angel looked at me. I felt tingly and excited and shy at the same time.

She brushed her hair away from her face. "C'mere, Glenda," she whispered.

There were two things I learned to open my mouth to do that summer: sing and kiss. I really can't say which one has served me better in life. If somebody told me today there could be no more singing and no more kissing, you could look for my body in the nearest river.

Angel and I kissed all night long. We kissed till the sunlight poured into her bedroom window and till our lips were so swollen and dry we had to put salve on them. We didn't stop kissing until Angel's mama knocked on the door and said it was time to wake up and get ready for church. We didn't really think that anybody would see a contradiction between us kissing all night and then going to church that morning. It made perfect sense to us. We loved each other, and we loved Jesus.

The trouble started the night Brother Dixon asked me about getting baptized. Angel and me were sitting in her kitchen eating milk and bread when Brother Dixon came in, looking all serious. "Miss Glenda, I was just sittin' in there readin' my Scripture, like I do of a night," he said, "when all of a sudden I got to thinkin' that I don't know if you have been baptized."

A clump of corn bread hung in my throat. "What do you mean, Brother Dixon?"

"Well, I was just thinkin' you'uns had been out of a pastor for two years before I come here, hadn't you?"

"Yessir."

"And I was just thinkin' that Angel didn't get baptized till she was ten year old, and that was with her livin' with a preacher all her life. So that got me to wonderin' if you ever got the chance to get yourself baptized."

I pushed away my bowl of milk and bread. "No, sir." To tell the truth, I had been secretly glad when the old preacher had left because I knew that if he hadn't, I would have had to get baptized sooner or later. You see, I'm scared to death of water. Always have been, always will be. I can't swim a lick to this day. And in Argon they didn't do baptisms in big old bathtub things like they do nowadays. They dunked you in the river.

"Well then," Brother Dixon said, smiling real big. "I reckon we're gonna have to get you baptized. I know you've already give your heart to Jesus, so there ain't no reason to beat around the bush. Ain't that right?"

I looked over at Angel. If I refused to get baptized, her daddy wouldn't let us be friends anymore. If I'd've jumped in a river for anybody, it would have been for Angel. "Yessir," I said.

"Praise Jesus!" he shouted, making me jump. "Well, I'll tell you what, Miss Glenda. There's a coupla people I'm baptizin' next Sunday. Why don't you join in with us?"

"Sure."

The rest of that week I tried to push the baptism into the back of my mind. At the time, I thought I was just scared of the water, but the idea of giving over my life to Jesus probably scared me, too. Maybe even then I wanted my life to be my life, not Jesus' or anybody else's.

Angel went with Roy and Vaughn and Bobby and me when we went to sing that Wednesday night, which turned out to be the only time we went somewhere to sing and didn't do it.

All we knew about this church was that it was way back in a holler. The preacher, a little rat-faced man, had heard us at a camp meeting and invited us to come and be special guest singers at his church. As it turned out, it didn't hardly look like a church at all; it was more like a fair-sized tar-paper shack.

There wasn't a sign on the building or anything, just a big cross made out of nailed-together pieces of scrap lumber.

Inside, though, it was packed. There weren't any real pews, just backless homemade benches with people sitting so close together on them that you wondered if they weren't committing some kind of sin. The little rat-faced preacher was already up front, holding forth on how the flames of hell would eternally scorch the skin of the wicked, although he did give Roy and Vaughn and me a friendly nod when he saw us. All the benches were full, so Roy and Vaughn just leaned up against the wall, and Angel and me sat down on a big wooden box at the back of the room.

That preacher was more in love with the sound of his own voice than anybody I had ever heard. He jumped and he paced and he banged his fist on the broken-down pulpit, hollering "Praise the Lord!" and "God's a good God, ain't he?" Angel leaned over to my ear and whispered, "Well, he seems awful excited about somethin', but I'll be dadblamed if I can figure out what he's preachin' on."

He kept talking and talking, and we were getting real antsy to get called up to sing. I was shifting my behind around on that hard wooden box, Vaughn was biting his fingernails, and Roy was jangling the change in his pockets. Had the preacher forgotten about us?

We never found out the answer because after about fifteen more minutes of ranting and railing, Old Reverend Rat Face said, "And now, my brothers and sisters, we have come to the time when we will test our faith. And as our Lord has commanded us, we shall take up serpents." He paused and looked at Angel and me. "If you young ladies would get offa that box of snakes, please."

We got off that box all right. It was like pulling your fingers off a red-hot stove — you don't even think about it; you just do it and do it as fast as you can. We were off that box and out the door and in the car, screaming our heads off all the way. Roy and Vaughn were right behind us. It's a wonder they even remembered to grab their guitars.

"Let's get the hell out of here, Bobby," Roy said. "Buncha crazy-ass holy rollers." He turned around to smile at Angel and me. "You girls didn't pee yourselves, didja?"

"Would you blame us if we did?"

He grinned. "Can't say as I would, Sissy. Can't say as I would."

The car peeled out of the holler and back onto the road home. "So, Bobby," Vaughn said, "you got any of that whiskey left? I reckon them snake handlers just about scared me sober."

We laughed the rest of the way home, teasing each other about who had been in the biggest hurry to get out of there. It was funny, but there was something to it, too. After what would happen that Sunday, I always considered the trip to the serpent-handling church sort of an omen. There I had been, thinking I was all safe and secure with Angel, when all the time we had been sitting on a big box of snakes.

I spent the night before my baptism with Angel. The plan was that I'd go down to the river with the Dixons in the morning, and my family would meet us there. I don't know what got into Angel and me that night, but as soon as the lights were off, that girl was on me like a duck on a june bug. We did a lot more than kiss like people in the movies.

"Take your nightgown off, Glenda," Angel whispered.

I figured, why not? All my sins would be washed away in the morning anyhow. I pulled off my gown and watched as Angel pulled hers off. Her red hair fell over her creamy shoulders that looked almost blue in the moonlight. And unlike me, she was already getting a good start in the bosom department.

Oh, it was heaven to kiss like that, bare chest to bare chest, belly to belly, thigh to thigh. We didn't really know to do much else but take turns lying on top of each other and kissing, but oh, that was enough. That was plenty.

We must have finally just wore each other out kissing, because the next thing I knew Brother Dixon was swinging the door open and hollering, "Hurry up, girls, you'll be late for chur —" He never finished the word *church* because what he saw in his daughter's bedroom must of made him think he had walked right into Sodom and Gomorrah.

I think he and I saw Angel's nightgown at the same time. It was crumpled up on the floor right next to his foot. I looked over at Angel, and sure enough, there she was, with not a stitch on but the quilt she was holding to cover herself. I spotted my gown at the foot of the bed and yanked it on as fast as I could. Brother Dixon slung Angel's gown at her, and turned to face me. His hair was the color of hellfire, and his eyes were the color of brimstone. "You — you whore!" he bellowed. "No, worse than a whore — Even a whore wouldn't lay down with her own kind!"

Before I knew what had hit me, Brother Dixon had lifted me out of the bed, thrown me out of Angel's room, and slammed the door. As I lay in a heap on the floor, I heard the girl I loved scream, "No, Daddy, no!" Then I heard the slaps.

"You think you're too old to whip, you little hussy?" Brother Dixon roared. "Well, you know what the Good Book says, 'Spare the rod, and spoil the child'!" Then I heard it again. Slap!

I was up on my feet, ready to break the door down if I had to save my precious Angel from that crazy man passing himself off as a preacher. Just as I slammed my body against the door, a pair of arms grabbed me from behind. I broke loose and wheeled around to see Mrs. Dixon, her eyes welled with tears.

"How —" I started, having to choke down a sob, "How can you let him hit her like that?"

Mrs. Dixon looked at me like she didn't even understand the question. "He's the man, Glenda. He knows best. Someday you'll understand." She flinched a little when she heard the scream coming from behind the locked door. "Now you go on and get cleaned up. We've got to be headin' down to the river."

My stomach knotted in fear. I had forgotten that Brother Dixon was supposed to baptize me that morning.

I walked to the river like a condemned woman. Nobody said a word, and Angel wouldn't look at me. Her freckled cheeks were red from her daddy's slaps, and she was walking like her behind hurt.

Mama and Daddy and Roy and Vaughn were already down at the river when we got there. So were the other two who were supposed to be baptized and their people. I wonder now why I didn't run right over to Mama and tell her something, anything, to get me away from that river and Brother Dixon. Maybe I thought I deserved to be punished. Maybe I didn't want to leave Angel alone with him. Or maybe I was just too scared to move.

For whatever reason it was, I just stood there like Joan of Arc or somebody while everybody prayed and sang "Shall We Gather at the River." When Brother Dixon waded out into the water and reached for the first victim, Daisy Adkins, an older lady who was rededicating her life to Jesus, I wished that a lightning bolt would strike me dead, that anything would happen to keep me from having to get into that water.

Daisy Adkins' baptism went fine. Brother Dixon just said, "I baptize you in the name of the Father, the Son, and the Holy Spirit," put a hanky over her nose, and dunked her real quick. He did the same with Old Man Cooper, the next baptizee. I prayed I would be so lucky.

Brother Dixon grabbed me by the wrist and yanked me waist deep into the muddy water. His hand was cold and bony, and he was squeezing my wrist so hard I thought he would break it. *Please, Jesus,* I prayed. *Please, Jesus, just a quick dip in the name of the Father, Son, and Holy Spirit, and I'll never kiss a girl again.*

Brother Dixon squeezed my wrist tighter, which I didn't even think was possible. When I looked up at him, his face was hot pink and the veins in his forehead were bulging out. "We have before us a sinner," he boomed. Everybody looked real surprised, especially my mama, who was probably wondering what I did wrong besides talk too much. "A sinner in the eyes of God," Brother Dixon went on, "a sinner in the eyes of this whole church!" He grabbed me by the shoulders and bored into me with those coal-black eyes. "But you are lucky, Glenda Mooney, lucky because you now stand before Jesus Christ who has the strength and the power — yes, the power! — to wash away the blackest of sins and make your nasty, stinkin' soul pure again!"

He didn't dunk me so much as tackle me. The first think I knew, his weight was on me, my head was under, and brown, brown water filled up my eyes and nose and mouth.

I knew I had to do something fast, so I grabbed on to his hand, twisted my head around, and bit him as hard as I could. He snatched his hand away, and I managed to get my head above water long enough to hear Old Man Cooper shout, "Praise the Lord! That demon's done left her body and gone into his'n!"

I was too busy coughing and spluttering to move fast, and Brother Dixon managed to grab ahold of my arm, shouting, "Don't you think you're pure yet, missy!"

Just then I heard two splashes as Vaughn and Roy jumped into the water. Roy broke in between Brother Dixon and me like we were playing a game of Red Rover. Vaughn helped me out of the water while Roy slugged Brother Dixon so hard in the jaw that he fell sprawling back into the river. As soon as I hit shore, I fell to my knees and vomited mud.

That was the last day my family had any part of

the Argon Missionary Baptist Church. Mama and Daddy wrote my almost fatal baptism off to the fact that Brother Dixon "wasn't from around here," but Roy and Vaughn agreed with me that it was really because the good reverend was just as crazy as a bessbug.

Even as an adult, though, Roy remembers the day of my baptism with a crooked-mouthed grin. "Hit was a dream come true for me, Sissy," he said to me one time. "I'd always wanted to bust a preacher one in the chops."

Chapter 4

Angel and me kind of grew apart after my baptism. Well, she grew apart from me anyway. I never blamed her — not after the beating she got the morning her daddy found us together. I guess she figured she had to stay away from me for her own personal safety.

I was pining away. I wouldn't sing at the churches anymore because I didn't feel like singing or being in a church neither one, and Roy and Vaughn were mad at me for backing out of their money-making scheme. All I did for the rest of that summer was sit out on the porch — the porch where I'd been sitting the first time I saw Angel and the first time I sang. I kept hoping that if I sat there long enough something else wonderful would happen, that I'd get back something I'd lost.

One night Mama came out and sat with me. "I brung you a biscuit and molasses," she said. "I thought you might want it. You hardly ate no supper."

I didn't even look up.

"I'm real worried about you, Glenda Fay." She scooted her chair over closer to mine. "You know, honey, just cause of what happened down at the river, I don't want you to give up on Jesus."

I looked over at her face, which was all crinkled up with worry. I felt sorry for Mama right then because she was trying so hard to help me and couldn't. I may not have understood that much about myself back then, but I knew Mama understood even less. "Down at the store today they was sayin' the Dixons is movin' back to Harlan. I guess word got out that he ain't right in the head."

My heart fell down to the pit of my stomach. I had known that Angel was out of my life, but I had thought I would at least get to look at her sometimes — that she'd be in my grade in school, and I'd look across the room and see that pretty red hair and remember what it smelled like.

"You'll find other friends, Glenda Fay. I know you don't think so right now, but you will. They'll be plenty of other girlfriends, and pretty as you are, it won't be long till boys is beatin' down the door to court you."

"Mama, why don't you go on inside? I feel like bein' by myself a while."

Her face went all slack, and I could tell I'd hurt her feelings. But I had to be alone. The more she talked, the lower I sank. "Well, mind you come in before the skeeters eat you alive," she muttered. The screen door slammed behind her.

The noise startled me, what with me already being nervous, and I jumped right out of my chair. Once I was on my feet, I started walking. I walked off the porch and down the dirt road Angel and me had walked down our first day together. I walked to the store, where my daddy was sitting on the porch with a bunch of men who were drinking pop and playing checkers and laughing. Daddy was hunched over rolling a cigarette and didn't even see me.

I kept on walking. I didn't know where I was going; I just knew I had to go. I walked past the Argon Missionary Baptist Church and came to Angel's house. To my surprise, I didn't even stop a minute. I just kept on walking. I walked out of Argon proper, past all the shotgun houses where the miners' families lived, then across the railroad tracks to where there were just tar-paper shacks. Mama and Daddy would've killed me if they had known where I was, but I didn't care.

Then I heard it, steady like a heartbeat, da-*da*-da-da-dump. Da-*da*-da-da-dump. I followed the sound to the edge of the woods. There was an oak tree there, perfect for climbing, so I clumb up in it as high as I could go and looked down.

They were in the clearing — a group of about six black men. A big man was playing the guitar, making that da-*da*-da-da-dump over and over again, and the voice that came out of him was so deep and sad that I felt like he had lifted it right out of his soul. And the song that he sang was not about Jesus, like most of the songs I knew, but about loving a woman and losing her.

The thing is, you'd think a song like that would've just made me sadder, but no. My heart lifted right out of the pit of my stomach and sprouted wings and flew around above that tree like the very bluebird of happiness. There was release in that music. Hallelujah, I felt like shouting. Praise — praise who?

It was then I knew what was in me was not just the power of God, though maybe it did come from God. What I had in me was the power of music.

And so did this man who was singing. That music ripped through my veins, sank into my bones, and surged through me like a bolt of lightning. Praise who? Praise music! The music was in me, and I knew I had to go wherever it took me — which, right then, was home.

I clumb down from that tree and ran as fast as I could. I leaped over the railroad tracks and dashed past Angel's house, the church, and the store. When I got back on the porch, I was soaked with sweat and my heart was pounding da-*da*-da-da-dump in my chest, but I wasn't tired at all. I tore into the living room, and Mama looked up from her mending and said, "Glenda Fay, what the sam hill's got into you?"

I ran right past her. There it was, in the corner, right where I'd remembered it. I opened the case and lifted out Vaughn's gleaming Silvertone guitar. He wouldn't care. He never touched it anymore anyway. I held its neck in my left hand and rested its curve on my knee. It was a perfect fit.

Chapter 5

I took to that guitar like a newborn baby to its mama's milk. By the time I was fifteen year old, I could listen to a song once on the radio and pick up my guitar and play it straight through. It was no wonder I was good. Since that night I'd gone walking to the other side of the tracks, play guitar was all I had done.

I didn't try to make any new friends after Angel left because I figured any girl I'd take up with would just be a cheap substitute. And since Mama had predicted that boys would be beating down my door, I made it a point never to give any old pimply-faced boy the time of day. Mama said that maybe I shouldn't play so hard to get. I said, "Mama, I don't just want to be hard to get. I want to be *impossible.*" No girlfriends and no boyfriends — that just left me and my guitar.

In school I'd sit quietly at my desk, listening to music in my head and dreaming of being a star on the one radio program I never missed. *Shady Grove Barn Dance* was broadcast live every Saturday night from Shady Grove, Kentucky, which was all the way up in the central part of the state.

Barn Dance was a country-Western music program, which featured old-timey fiddler Lonesome Joe Whitcomb, cowboy singer Rusty Perkins, and the hilarious country comedian Miz Lucindy, whose catch phrase "Well, I *swannn*" was repeated by listeners wherever the show was broadcast.

But what really got to me was the girl singer, Maggie Waters, who just moaned out these songs of heartbreak and abandonment. I'd close my eyes and picture her on stage in a shiny powder-blue evening gown, her brunet hair done in waves like a movie star's. I just heard her on the radio, so I didn't really have any idea what she looked like; that's just how I imagined her. And it didn't take long till I was imagining myself on that stage, moaning out those songs and wearing that beautiful gown.

I was living in a fantasy world in those days, just waiting for something fabulous to happen. Mama said I had gotten so dreamy I wasn't no good to nobody.

As it turned out, it was Roy who found a way to turn my dreams into reality. He had already dropped out of school by then and was working in the mines.

One evening I was sitting on the porch when he came running down the road. He had just got off work and was tar black from head to foot, the whites of his eyes the only white thing about him. I was scared because he was running. He usually dragged back from the mines bone tired like all the other men did. I jumped up and hollered, "Roy, is everything okay? There ain't been an accident or nothin'?"

He flopped down in a chair on the porch, pulled out his flask, and took a big swig. "Naw, Sissy," he said finally. "Hit's good news for a change. I reckon it's time for you to get offa this porch and run with the big dogs."

"What do you mean?"

"Well, some fellers was talkin' at dinnertime today about how the people from *Shady Grove Barn Dance* is comin' down to Morgan on Saturday. They go all over the place lookin' for talent, you know. They're havin' tryouts at Morgan High School for people to be on the show."

I couldn't believe it. Here before me was the opportunity to live my life in the present, not just spend all my time dreaming about the maybes of the future. "Roy, I've got to do this."

He grinned and patted me on the knee. "I know it, Sissy. I'll get you there. You just be thinkin' about what you want to sing."

The tryouts for *Barn Dance* were held in the auditorium of Morgan High School. When Roy and me got there, we quickly discovered that *everybody* wants to be on the radio. I had never seen so many people in one place. The auditorium was packed with town people and people from back in the mountains, most of them carrying guitar cases just like me. All of a sudden I felt very foolish. Here I had been thinking I was something special for wanting to be a singer, when all along I had really just wanted what everybody else did.

"Good god-a-mighty, Roy," I said. "Look at all them people."

"Aw, Sissy, I bet you sing better'n all of 'em put together."

My hands were sweaty, and I had to pee. "Roy, I don't think I can go through with this."

Roy looked at me real serious, which he hardly ever did. "Sissy, that's bullshit, and you know it. This is what you've wanted your whole life. Besides, I drove you all this way, and we ain't goin' nowhere till you've sung for these here people."

A woman in a neat little suit was sitting at a table at the entrance to the auditorium, and Roy shoved me toward her. I grabbed the edge of the table, trying not to fall right on top of her. "Are you here to audition, miss?" she asked.

Her professional manner and pink painted lips made me feel like the biggest hick that ever lived. I looked down at my homemade cotton dress and scuffed penny loafers. "Uh . . . I'm here to try out for *Barn Dance.*"

"Name, please?"

"Uh," I said, like I had to think for a minute before I could remember my own name, "Glenda Mooney."

"M-o-o-n-y?"

"E-y."

She wrote my name down at the end of a long list. "Have a seat in the auditorium, Miss Mooney, and I'll call your name when we're ready for you."

"Thank you." I wandered away from her table, realized I had left my guitar there, and rushed back to get it, feeling like an even bigger idiot.

Roy and me sat down in the back of the auditorium. "Lord," he said, "you sure are a nervous wreck."

"Tell me somethin' I don't know."

"Did you see that town girl that was standin' behind you, the one with the yeller hair?"

"Uh-uh." I was too wrapped up in being scared to notice anybody else.

"She sure was good-lookin'," Roy said. "She prob'ly goes to high school here. I bet she wouldn't give an old country boy like me the time of day."

I couldn't imagine going to a school as big as Morgan High. Argon had a three-room schoolhouse. Grades 1–4 were in one room, grades 5–8 in the next, and grades 9–12 in the next. The 9–12 room was almost empty, since by that time most of the boys had left school to work in the mines, and a lot of the girls had dropped out to get married. But Morgan High School seemed huge. The walls of the hall were lined with locker after locker, and the auditorium must have had at least two hundred seats. I shuddered, thinking that just about everybody else sitting in those seats was competing against me.

About that time, the woman from the table walked onto the stage, her high heels going click, click, click. "All right," she said into the microphone. "We're ready to begin. Please report to the stage when I call your name, and we ask that everyone limit his act to three minutes. Also, we ask audience members not to applaud, since applause slows down our proceedings."

Sometimes there wasn't even the temptation to applaud, like in the case of the woman with the beehive hairdo who bellowed out "Rock of Ages" like a mule in pain. Or there was the old man who seemed to think he should be on the radio because he could spit his tobacco clear across the stage and hit a bull's-eye with it. It wasn't that this wasn't a talent; it was just a talent that would lose something over the radio.

The best singing I heard was from Emily Cole, the yellow-haired girl Roy liked. When her name was called, she walked up on the stage and sang "Wayfaring Stranger" in a voice that flowed out as clear and pure as a mountain stream.

When my name was called, I spent what felt like years walking up to the stage. I had never performed on a real stage before, since I had just sung in little bitty churches. I never will forget the view from that stage — the rows and rows of faces just waiting to see what I would do, waiting to see if I was any good or not. The lady who had called my name sat in the front row with a big man in a white suit and a skinny man wearing a Western-style shirt and scarf. I knew they were the judges, and I knew I had better be good.

I was. I strapped on my guitar, leaned into the mike, and tore into "Goin' Down the Road Feelin' Bad." My voice might not have been as clear and bubbly as the yellow-haired girl's, but it was packed with emotion — emotion that spilled out of my mouth and tingled in my fingers as they picked the guitar strings. I looked out at the audience, and I knew I had them. If it'd been church, they'd have been speaking in tongues.

Well, all except the judges. It was hard to tell about them. They were busily scribbling away on their clipboards, and when I wound the song up, all the lady said was thank you, which was what she had said to everybody else.

After the last person had tried out, the lady announced that the judges would have made their decisions in half an hour, if we would care to wait. If we would care to wait! Like we were going to go to all the trouble of trying out and then not stay to find out whether or not we made it. The three judges trooped out of the auditorium, and everybody else started stirring around and talking nervously.

"Sissy, come outside with me while I smoke a cigarette," Roy said.

I followed him without saying a word. I was a nervous wreck. I couldn't stop thinking how awful it would be if I didn't get chosen. To have gotten a taste of real performing and then to have to go back to Argon and daydream while I helped Mama with the chores . . . it would be too cruel.

"You're white as a sheet, Sissy. You all right?"

"Just nervous is all."

"I don't see what you got to be nervous about. You and that Emily girl was the best'uns up there."

"But what if they've got to choose between her and me? Who would you pick?"

Roy grinned. "Now, Sissy, you should never ask a man to choose between his own sister and a yeller-haired town girl." He pulled his flask out of his pocket and, to my surprise, held it out to me. "Here, have you a sup of this. It'll calm your nerves."

I unscrewed the lid and held the bottle up to my nose.

"Hit ain't aftershave, Sissy. Don't smell it; drink it."

I took a swallow and felt a slow, comfortable burn creep down from my tongue to my throat to my belly. I took another swallow.

"Now, now, Sissy. I said have a sup, not the whole bottle. You don't wanna go back in there a-staggerin', do you?"

When a slow half hour had passed, everybody filed back into the building like cows lining up to be slaughtered. Once everybody was in their seats, the lady in the suit walked back up on stage, clutching her clipboard. "First," she said, "let me introduce our judges, *Barn Dance* regulars Lonesome Joe Whitcomb and Rusty Perkins." The man in the white suit and the man in the Western shirt turned around and waved. I couldn't believe I had played for people I had listened to on the radio every Saturday night of my life.

The lady continued, "And I am Eva Mitchell, stage manager and general secretary for *Barn Dance.* I would like to say that we truly enjoyed all the performances today. Unfortunately for most of you, only three of today's performers were selected as *Barn Dance* material."

All of a sudden it felt like there was no air left in the room because everybody had sucked in their breath at the same time.

She cleared her throat. "The three performers chosen were Billy Joe Macon . . ." He deserved it. He was a real good mandolin player. "Emily Cole . . ." I knew they'd pick her instead of me. I clapped anyway. After all, she could sing. "And Glenda Mooney." For a second, I clapped like Glenda Mooney was somebody else. Then I realized it was me. It was me! I hugged Roy. I was still warm from the whiskey and was laughing and crying at the same time, I was so happy.

Miss Mitchell continued, "Those whose names I just called, please stay and talk with us. Everyone else is free to go. Thank you for your time."

The people who didn't get picked got out awful fast. I heard the tobacco-spitting man yell, "I'm never gonna listen to that sonuvabitch Joe Whitcomb on the radio again!"

"That's nothin'!" another man hollered. "I'm goin' home and bustin' my radio!"

Roy told me he'd wait outside, and soon it was just Billy Joe Macon, Emily Cole, the judges, and me. "All right, kids," Lonesome Joe Whitcomb barked, "Get up front here so I can look at you'uns." We did as we were told. "Now what most people who listen to *Shady Grove Barn Dance* don't know is that I own it. I started *Barn Dance,* and I'm the one that does all the hirin' and firin'. You work hard, you do what I tell you, you keep your job. Understand?"

"Yessir," we all said together.

"All right, then. Miss Mitchell's got your contracts. We'll start you each off with twenty dollars a week. You'll need to report to work on the fifth of April, so wrap up any business here before then. We'll find you'uns a place to stay when ya get there, so don't worry none about that. At *Shady Grove Barn Dance,* we're all one big ol' family, and I believe in seein' that my young'uns gets taken care of." His lips spread into a toothy grin. "All right, then. Let's get them contracts signed."

Roy took me to the Dixie Diner to celebrate. It was the first time I had eaten in a restaurant. There weren't any restaurants in Argon, and besides, Daddy always said eating out was a waste of money. I was so excited I giggled when the waitress brought me my Coke. Here I was, sitting in a restaurant in town, about to be a star on *Shady Grove Barn Dance.* I had two chili dogs, a bag of potato chips, and a fried apple pie. It was the best food I had ever eaten.

Chapter 6

Since you're an educated person, you probably think Mama and Daddy pitched a fit when I told them I was quitting school to join *Barn Dance.* But the truth is, they never batted an eye. Kids were always dropping out of school in Argon, boys to work in the mines and girls to get married, so at least me dropping out to be on the radio was something different. Not that Mama and Daddy said they were proud of me either. They were mountain people, and most mountain people don't let themselves get all excited over things, good or bad.

Mountain girl or not, I was excited. All my life, I had wanted to be something better than a miner's wife cooped up all day in a little coal dust–covered shotgun house. And that April morning after I'd turned sixteen, when Roy and Vaughn drove me to catch the nine A.M. Greyhound bus out of Morgan to Shady Grove, I knew I was headed for something better. Or at least something different, which, at the time, was good enough for me.

The bus ride to Shady Grove took almost four and a half hours. By car it would have taken no more than three, but of course a bus has to stop at every little pig path along the way so people can get on and off. I sat next to an old lady who was going to Harroldsburg to see her sister in the hospital. "Bless her heart," she kept saying, "she ain't doin' a bit of good."

When she asked me where I was going I held up my guitar case and said I was going to Shady Grove to be on the radio. The old lady cackled and slapped her thigh. "Oh, tell me another'n," she laughed. "Tell me another'n!"

Miss Mitchell met me at the Shady Grove bus station wearing a smart custardy yellow spring suit. "I trust you had a pleasant trip, Glenda."

"Yes'm."

"Well, most of our new performers stay over at Irma Willard's boarding house. It's right across the street from *Barn Dance,* which makes it particularly convenient if you don't have a car. Also, Mrs. Willard gives *Barn Dance* members a special deal on rent. Does that sound agreeable to you?"

"Yes'm." It was my first time away from home, and I was so green that if Miss Mitchell had told me I should live on a flat rock, I'd've done it.

As it turned out, Mrs. Willard's place — and Mrs. Willard — were real nice. The boarding house was a big white saltbox house with rocking chairs on the front porch that gave it a real homey look. Mrs. Willard was a big, blousy, middle-aged woman who peroxided her hair and looked like she had been born with a cigarette in her hand. "Well, look at you, young'un," she said as soon as she saw me. "I reckon we're gonna have to fatten you up so you can fill out them pretty dresses you'll be wearin' on *Barn Dance.* How old are you, hon?"

"Sixteen."

"Sixteen, huh? Well, I'll just put you in the room next to mine — keep them boys that lives here from gettin' any ideas. Now . . . you ain't the type who wants the boys to get ideas, are you?"

"No, ma'am," I said, with more confidence than I'd said anything else since I'd hit Shady Grove.

"Well, good. This is a respectable house, you know. They's been some girls come here, and Lord, you woulda thought it was a different kinda house altogether!"

Miss Mitchell laughed and said, "Well, Glenda, I think you're in good hands. Come over to the Barn at seven-thirty; we have free tickets to the show for all the new performers. Afterward we'll take you backstage to meet everybody, and I think Lonesome Joe wants to say a few words to the young'uns, as he calls you. So . . . I'll see you around seven-thirty."

"Thank you, ma'am." I felt like I had stepped out of my life and into somebody else's. In just a few hours I was going to be watching *Shady Grove Barn Dance.* In just a few days, I'd be performing on it.

"Good lord, hon, you look like you've been poleaxed," Mrs. Willard said. "Now, do you want me to show you your room or not?"

"Oh, yes'm. Sorry." I picked up my guitar case and my little cardboard suitcase and followed her up the stairs.

"You're a guitar player, huh?" she said. "My husband played guitar on *Barn Dance* before he passed on. Seems like I've spent my whole life lookin' after guitar players."

The room was plain — a narrow maple bed, a matching dresser, a beat-up rocking chair by a window with homemade white curtains. It was plain but clean, and it was mine. I had never had a room all to myself before. It felt good.

"You think you can live here, hon?"

"Oh, yes, ma'am. It's a lot nicer than what I'm used to."

"Well, that's good, I reckon. You're movin' up in the world, then. The bathroom's down the hall on the right. Clean the tub after you're through."

"Yes'm."

"Breakfast's at seven-thirty, dinner's at twelve-thirty, and supper's at five-thirty. I expect to see you there. Like I said, we've got to put some meat on them bones."

It was funny the trouble I went to getting settled because I didn't hardly have anything to unpack: three dresses besides the one I had on, a nightgown, some socks and underwear, a hairbrush, a toothbrush, a bar of soap, and a bottle of shampoo. That was all I had, but I took forever arranging everything just so: folding and refolding my clothes and putting them in drawers, arranging my few toiletry items carefully on my dresser. Shoot, I even folded my underwear! It seems silly now, but at the time, it seemed so important to have my own place and my own things just the way I wanted them. Privacy is one of life's greatest luxuries, and that little room in Mrs. Willard's boarding house gave me my first taste of it.

At *Barn Dance,* I sat next to Emily Cole, the yellow-haired girl from Morgan that Roy liked so much. I was so excited about the show I could hardly stay in my seat. I leaned over to Emily to try to start a conversation. "I can't believe I'm finally gonna get to see what all these people I've heard on the radio look like."

"Oh, you've never seen the show before?"

"Uh-uh. Have you?"

She tossed her hair like a bored princess. "Oh, Daddy's brought me here a bunch of times. I've been to the *Opry,* too."

Since I didn't want to reveal that before that day the farthest I had traveled from Argon was to Morgan, I decided to change the subject. "I thought you sung real good at the tryouts."

You would think she would've said something nice about my singing then, even if it was only to be polite, but instead she said, "Well, I *am* the soloist at the Morgan First Baptist Church. My daddy's the pastor there, you know."

A voice in my head said, *She's a preacher's daughter — get the hell away from her.* But the auditorium was so packed that there was no place to go but out, and there was no way I was going to miss the show.

I was saved from having to talk to Emily any more because right then the lights went out and Lonesome Joe Whitcomb's voice started reciting the show's introduction just like I had heard it on the radio every Saturday night I could remember:

Paws and maws and young'uns, too,
Put away your chores and kick off your shoes.
Get your toes to tappin' and your mouth set to grin,
'Cause *Shady Grove Barn Dance* is about to begin!

It was like magic. The lights on the stage came on, and there, standing in front of the bales of hay and old-timey farm tools, was Lonesome Joe Whitcomb and his band. He started fiddling and the band kicked in, and that music just filled me up inside till I felt like getting up and dancing. But the funny thing was, even though it was called a barn dance, nobody danced. There was no place to dance, really, so everybody just sat in their seats. When I listened on the radio, I always thought there'd be dancing.

But Lonesome Joe and his band weren't even the best part. Maggie Waters came out and sang "Heartbreakin' Man" in a voice that was so sad and sweet that I broke out in goose bumps all over. Maggie Waters wasn't like I had pictured her at all, though. She was shorter and rounder than the glamour girl I had thought her to be, but in her own way, she was even more beautiful than I had imagined her. I still would've put her in a powder-blue evening gown, though, instead of the yellow gingham frock she had on. But it wouldn't really have mattered if she had been wearing a flour sack; her voice was perfect.

Once she finished singing, Lonesome Joe came on stage and took her hand. "I hate to tell you folks this," he said, "But this will be the last night Maggie Waters performs on *Barn Dance.* Some ol' boy come along and stole her away from us, and now she's thinkin' she wants to have her some babies to sing to. So, Maggie, God bless you, honey, and all of us here at *Barn Dance* wish you all the happiness in the world. Folks, put your hands together for Miss Maggie Waters before she runs off and becomes a Mrs."

Everybody stood up and clapped. I felt like I was going to cry because I had so hoped I would be working with Maggie Waters and because I couldn't understand how she could just up and quit being a radio star to get married and have babies. Would she miss the applause? Nobody gives you a standing ovation for changing a diaper.

I couldn't be sad for long, though, because after Maggie Waters left the stage, Lonesome Joe introduced "that little gal from up on Possum Creek, here with all the latest gossip, Miz Lucindy Jane!"

Miz Lucindy strutted out then. She was a sight to see — a strapping girl with long, honey-blonde hair in pigtails and a big, gap-toothed grin. She had on a real tacky flowered dress, a bunch of dime-store jewelry, and the awfullest pair of clodhoppers you ever did see. She stepped up to the microphone and looked around wide-eyed at the audience. "Well, I *swannn,*" she hollered, and everybody laughed and clapped. "I don't reckon I've seen so many people in one place since the church picnic where Cousin Boyce spiked the watermelon with moonshine!"

She grinned while everybody laughed. "Well, I like to forgot to tell you about what happened to my uncle Devoy. You'uns knows my uncle Devoy, don'tcha?" Applause. "Well, the Yankee county extension agent come over to Uncle Devoy's farm the other day, said he wanted to look at Uncle Devoy's hogs. Uncle Devoy said, 'Wellsir, I was just about to take my hogs down to the crick for water, so I reckon you can come with me.' Now Uncle Devoy has him ten hogs. So first he took out one hog, and he walked him down to the crick for water. Then he walked that hog back and took out the old sow and walked her down to the crick for water. He kept doin' that, you know, takin' the hogs out one by one and walkin' them to the crick and then back to the pen. By the seventh hog, that county extension agent was gettin' purty tired of walkin' back and forth. So he turned to my uncle Devoy and said, 'Wouldn't it save a lot of time if you just took all the hogs out at once?' My uncle Devoy says, 'Wellsir, I don't see as how it makes no differnce. Time don't mean nothin' to a hog.' "

I laughed till I was about to bust. Miz Lucindy put me in mind of so many people I knew back in Argon. I couldn't wait to meet her.

After the show, I had my chance. Miss Mitchell came and got Emily and Billy Joe and some other new hires I hadn't met yet and me and took us backstage. We got clapped on the back by band members who said things like "glad to have you aboard." I was so carried away with being backstage at *Barn Dance* that I walked smack into this tall woman wearing a tailored tweed suit. "Oh, I'm sorry," I said.

She stooped down, muttering, "Dropped my goddamn cigarette." It was then I recognized who it was. The accent was completely different, but the hair was the right shade of blonde and the gap between the two front teeth was there.

"Why, you're Miz Lucindy!" I squealed. "Oh, I just *love* you. You just put me in mind of so many people from back home —"

She looked at Miss Mitchell, who was standing next to me. "Who's the rube?" she growled.

"Susan, this is Glenda Mooney, one of our new hires. Glenda, this is Susan Wilson. She *plays* Miz Lucindy."

"Well, good luck to you, kid. You'll need it. This place is a friggin' madhouse." She stalked off, leaving me standing there slack-jawed like, like a rube.

Miss Mitchell draped her arm around me. "Glenda, I think Mr. Whitcomb wanted to talk to you and Emily in his dressing room."

She knocked on the door for us. Lonesome Joe answered, wearing his white pants with just an undershirt. Miss Mitchell nudged us through the door. "How you doin', Sweetie and Salty?"

"Beg pardon?" I said.

"Sweetie and Salty," he boomed. "I've been thinkin' about you girls's singin'. Miz Emily, you've got a real sweet voice — sweet as molasses — and you, Miz Glenda, you've got a salty voice. You know, hit's got a little bite to it. So," he said, "I think I know what to do with that combination. Y'all are gonna sing together. Sweetie and Salty Cole, the Cole Sisters!"

"But we're not sisters," Emily said in a tone that made me think she didn't like me any more than I liked her.

"Oh, that don't matter. All that matters is that the audience thinks you're sisters."

"But I was kinda hopin' to use my own name," I said.

"Honey, hit don't matter if it's your name or not. It'll still be your voice, won't it?"

"Well . . ."

"Trust me on this, girls. I've been in this business since I was younger than you'uns. I know a sister act when I see one, and you, girls, are the Cole Sisters."

I looked at my new sister and smiled uneasily. The sibling rivalry was about to begin.

Chapter 7

You should have seen what they made us wear. As soon as Lonesome Joe had given Emily and me our new identities, he told the *Barn Dance* seamstress to run us up some matching outfits. And sure enough, by the next morning, we each had a frilly checked-gingham pinafore, Emily's in pink-and-white and mine in blue-and-white. We wore them in rehearsal that day, and Emily actually looked all right. The pink went good with her rosy cheeks and yellow hair, and she was the kind of girl that could wear frills without making a fool of herself. I, on the other hand, was something to see. With my dark hair pulled into pigtails and my blue checked dress, I looked like I'd made a wrong turn following the yellow brick road. This was not the glamorous look I had hoped for.

But the outfits were just one part of Lonesome Joe's evil plan. He also thought we should both play guitars, which was fine by me, but Emily couldn't play a lick.

"Well, honey," Lonesome Joe said, grinning at Emily the way dirty old men grin at pretty blonde girls, "I reckon you can just kindly act like you're strummin' on it, and ol' Salty can do the real playin'."

Needless to say, I wasn't real happy with this arrangement. I had already written my parents to tell them I'd be performing under Emily's last name so they'd know me when they heard me on the radio. Now it turned out that I was going to be the one playing the music, and old Princess Sweetie would still get all the glory. I wondered if it would make any difference if I learned to bat my eyelashes at Lonesome Joe like she did. Probably not. Some girls can pull off that kind of thing, but girls like me know better than to try.

That afternoon when rehearsal let out, I decided to go for a walk. I hadn't really explored the town of Shady Grove yet, and besides, I needed to be by myself, to feel like Glenda Mooney instead of this new Salty Cole person. I walked past the Barn and the boarding house, heading toward town.

As it turned out, town was farther away than I thought. I kept walking and walking, expecting to see civilization, but all I saw was fields of cows. All of a sudden I heard a whirring sound and turned around to see a car unlike any I had ever seen. It was a brand-new convertible, as shiny and red as a just-picked apple. It slowed to a stop, and behind the wheel, wearing cat's-eye sunglasses, was Miz Lucind . . . Susan Wilson. She pushed her glasses down on her nose to get a better look at me. "Hey — it's, uh, Wendy, right?"

"Glenda."

"Oh, yeah. Of course, old Tiresome Joe is making you go by some god-awful stage name, isn't he?"

I grinned embarrassedly. "Yeah, Salty Cole. Ain't that the most harebrained name you ever heard?"

Her laugh was low and gravelly. "No, dear. Miz Lucindy Jane is the most harebrained name I ever heard. Joe came up with that one, too."

Suddenly it occurred to me that the two of us were having a friendly conversation not twenty-four hours after she had cut me dead backstage. "I don't want you to take this the wrong way, Miz Wilson, but why are you bein' nice to me?"

She laughed again. "Well, no one could accuse you of beating around the bush." She took a cigarette from her jacket pocket and lit it with a flick of a silver lighter. "Look, Glenda, I didn't mean to be rude yesterday. I was just having a really bad day. I had just gotten the curse, my mother had called to tell me what a disappointment I was, and one of the boys in the band had just grabbed my ass. You have to watch those musicians, Glenda; they'll be all over you at the drop of a hat."

My jaw must've been down to the ground right then. I had never heard a girl talk so openly about her monthly visitor, let alone complain about her mama. I didn't know what to say, so I didn't say anything.

"In case you couldn't tell, Glenda, that was my apology. Miss Mitchell told me to apologize, and so I just did." She sighed like politeness was a strain for her. "So are you going to accept it or not?"

"Accept what?"

"My apology, for crissakes."

"Oh, yeah, sorry."

"You don't know what the hell to make of me, do you, kid?"

"Well, I've never met nobody like you before."

She whooped with laughter, slapping the steering wheel. "I bet that's the truth! Say, where are you going?"

"No place special. I was just walkin'."

"Well, no need to walk when you can ride. I'm going downtown to the liquor store. Wanna come?"

I don't even remember making a conscious decision. I just hopped in before Susan had a chance to change her mind.

It was like I was in a movie, sitting in this shiny red car next to this gorgeous woman. The April breeze was blowing through my hair, and I couldn't believe my life at that moment. Only a couple of months before, when it had been a cold, gray winter in Argon and I had been wrapped up in a quilt in front of the coal stove trying to get warm, nothing like this had seemed possible. That perfect moment, on the road to Shady Grove with Susan, is what I always think of when I hear the word *spring*.

Downtown Shady Grove was bigger than Argon, but that was about all you could say for it. There was a grocery store, a drug store, a five-and-dime, and a post office. On the edge of town was the liquor store, or the package store, as its sign said.

"You want anything?" Susan asked as she parked in front of the store.

"I'm just sixteen," I said.

"I didn't ask how old you are. I asked you if you wanted anything."

"Uh, I guess not." I didn't really know what to ask for. The only liquor I had ever drunk was from my brother's flask, and I had a feeling it probably wasn't store-bought.

A couple of minutes later, Susan strode out of the store carrying a bottle wrapped up in a brown paper bag. "I have just purchased a fifth of very high-quality bourbon. You're more than welcome to come back to my apartment and sample it. Of course, if you're going to chicken out on me, you have to come up with a better excuse than your tender age."

"What do you want to drink with me for? I thought you said I was a rube."

"Well, you are, but you seem like you could be a fun rube. Not like that Bible-thumping little Goody Two-shoes Tiresome Joe's trying to pass off as your sister."

I laughed. "It just ain't fair, you know. All my life I wanted a sister I could talk to, and now here I am, stuck with Emily Cole. I reckon it's true what they say — 'Be careful what you wish for; it just might come true.' "

Susan grinned, showing that little gap between her front teeth. "Glenda, let's you and me go have a drink."

Susan's apartment was just above the dry goods store. It was small, just one room with a kitchenette and a little bathroom, but the furniture and decorations were nice — nicer than any I had seen before. She had a brand-new couch, the kind that folds out into a bed, and a kidney-shaped coffee table that had a bunch of magazines stacked on it. Not cheap movie magazines like Mama read sometimes, but sophisticated ones like *Vanity Fair* and *The New Yorker.* There was a bookcase just brimming with books, and — this is what really got my attention — a real phonograph and a whole stack of records.

"You've got a record player!" I squealed, forgetting to act cool.

"Look through the records if you want. We can listen to anything you like."

I touched the records as carefully as if they had been made of fine crystal. I had never even held a record in my hands, and just the thought that something as personal as music could be captured on these little disks of vinyl thrilled and baffled me. Here were all these new voices and new sounds. I didn't know where to begin.

Susan handed me a glass. "You've even got records by colored people!" I said.

"Yes," she laughed, probably amused at how impressed I was with something she took for granted. "Say, have you ever heard Billie Holiday?"

"I've never even heard of him."

"*Her,* actually." She riffled through the stack of albums. "Yes, I think you need to hear this."

We sat in silence and listened. Her voice was smooth and hot and cool at the same time, like the iced bourbon that was sliding down my throat. When the record was over, I said, "What kind of music is that?"

Susan purred out the word: *Jazz.*

"Jazz," I echoed back. Liking the way it felt to say it, I said it again. "Jazz."

After that, she put on some music by Mozart. "Now, this is classical music," she said. "That means that the man who wrote it has been dead for a long time."

This music was light and airy like the feeling I was getting in my head from drinking the bourbon. I found myself giggling all of a sudden.

"What is it, Glenda?"

"Oh, nothin'. It's just that I was thinkin' you ain't nothin' like Miz Lucindy."

"No, Miz Lucindy's just a character I play. She's not my favorite character either. She gets on my nerves, but God love her, she pays the rent, so I can't complain much. I feel like a kept woman sometimes — kept by Miz Lucindy."

"You don't like playin' her?"

"No, not really." Susan got up from the couch, got the bottle of bourbon from the kitchen counter, and moved it to the coffee table in front of us. "I'm a real actress, you know. I have a degree in theater from Midland College. Do you know Midland?"

"Can't say as I do." My teachers at school were the only people I knew who'd been to college, and they'd just been to the state teachers' college.

"Oh, it's a snotty little junior college for snotty little rich girls. You can actually board your horse on campus. You see, Glenda, I'm not a rube; I'm a snotty little rich girl. Or at least that's what I was brought up to be. But after college, instead of marrying some snotty little rich boy like I was supposed to, I ran off to New York to pursue my acting career." She drained her glass and poured more. "Which I did, for about a year, when the money ran out. Then it was back home to Mommy and Daddy, mucking out their stables and hearing constantly what a failure I was.

"But then I saw in the paper where they were looking for a country comedian at *Shady Grove Barn Dance,* and I figured what the hell? I can come up with something."

"So Miz Lucindy was who you came up with?"

"Yep. The old girl's my blessing and my curse. She keeps me independent of my parents, which is good. But all things being equal, I'd rather be playing Medea."

I didn't know Medea from a hole in the ground, so I just smiled and nodded.

"But you're lucky, Glenda. Why, I bet being on *Barn Dance* is what you've dreamed of your whole life."

I hated being so transparent. "Well, not like this," I said. "I wanted to be on it as Glenda Mooney, not half of a made-up sister act."

"And there it is," Susan said, pouring more bourbon into my glass. "Fame, even small-time fame, never comes the way we want it to. But . . ." She lifted her glass and clinked it against mine. "Here's to taking it any way we can get it, even if that means we make complete asses of ourselves."

There was a sadness to Susan that I couldn't figure out. Here she was, a famous comedian who had grown up with everything she could possibly want, and now she lived in a beautiful apartment full of records and books, and she still wasn't happy. I didn't know whether to hug her or slap her face.

The record ended, and she put a new one on the turntable. "This," she said, dropping the needle on the record, "this is the blues."

I recognized it. That steady da-*da*-da-da-dump I had heard that night in the woods, that low, moaning voice — except that this time it belonged to a woman. The blues. So that's what it was called. And women could do it, too. I sat and listened quietly, respectfully, like I was in church.

When the song was over, Susan softly breathed the name, "Bessie Smith."

I was full of music and bourbon, so I told her about how I used to think I was called to sing the Lord's music until that night in the woods when I heard the blues for the first time without even knowing what I was hearing, and how the holy spirit of music filled me up so much that I had to run home and steal my brother's guitar.

Susan reached over and patted my arm. I liked the way her hand felt on me. "You know, Salty Cole," she said, smiling, "you might not be such a rube after all."

We had drunk a lot without eating anything, so Susan said she would go whip us up an omelet, which turned out to be eggs scrambled up fluffy with ham and cheese in them. It was real good.

After we ate, Susan said, "You got a boyfriend back in — where is it that you're from?"

"Argon."

"Ah, yes. So, is there some little Billy Joe Jim Bob or somebody back there, waiting for you to come home and have his babies?"

I rolled my eyes. "Look, I've never cared much about boys — I mean, I love my brothers, and their friends is all right, too, but I've never cared nothin' about boys, you know, that way."

"Mm-hmm," Susan said, nodding. She seemed a million miles away for a second, then looked me so straight in the eye it just about made me nervous. She held up her left hand. On her pinkie was a simple little gold ring with an *S* engraved on it. "Glenda, do you know what this means?"

"What your hand means? A hand don't mean nothin'; it's just a hand."

"No, what this ring means."

I stared at the ring, not knowing what I was supposed to say.

Susan sighed. "Oh, of course you don't know what it means. I'll tell you someday." She stood up. "Well, that food sobered me up quite a bit. Why don't I drive you back to the boarding house?"

"Susan, tell me what it means," I whined. I was going crazy. I had failed her little test, and now I was a rube again.

"I'll tell you later. I believe you've had enough new experiences for today."

I tiptoed into the boarding house holding my shoes in my hand so I wouldn't make too much noise. I sneaked up the stairs and was turning the key in my door when the door to Mrs. Willard's room swung open. She was wearing a pink housecoat, and her hair was in curlers.

"There you are!" she said. "When you wasn't at supper, I thought you'd dropped off the face of the earth."

"I'm sorry, ma'am. I didn't mean to worry you."

"It ain't about worryin', Miss Glenda. You're a grown girl, and I ain't your mama. But you remember what I said about this bein' a respectable house. You can't live here if you're gonna run around with fellers all hours of the night."

"But Mrs. Willard, that wasn't what I was doin'."

"What do you mean?"

"I mean . . . I was out with a girl."

"Oh," Mrs. Willard said. "Well, I reckon there's no harm in that." She went back in her room and shut the door behind her.

Chapter 8

The first night we performed on *Barn Dance,* Lonesome Joe introduced us as "the sweethearts of *Shady Grove Barn Dance,* Sweetie and Salty Cole — the Cole Sisters!" The last thing I wanted to be was the sweetheart of anything, but when I walked out on stage, I was grinning like a possum and looking like I was so sweet you could just eat me up. Who'd have thought it? I wasn't just a singer; I was an actress, too!

We sang "Down in the Valley." That was the kind

of stuff Lonesome Joe wanted us to do — soft, slow mountain tunes. Emily and me did have good harmony together, even though off stage we tried to stay as far away from each other as possible. The audience loved us, which was thrilling. But even then, I knew the little mountain songbird bit wasn't me. It wasn't that I was doing a bad job. You can teach a dog to walk on his hind legs, and he can do it real good, but deep down he knows that ain't the way he was meant to walk. That was how it was with the kind of singing I was doing on *Barn Dance.* The trouble was, I didn't know what kind of singing I was meant to do.

When we walked off stage, Susan was in the wings, dressed as Miz Lucindy. It really was like they were two different people. She tugged on my pigtail. "You did good, kid," she whispered.

I grinned and walked on, since Lonesome Joe was introducing her. A minute later I learned why Susan had felt the need to warn me about the boys in the band. Jimmy, a banjo player, sidled up to me and put his arm around my waist. "So," he drawled, "I reckon if you're the sweetheart of *Barn Dance,* and I'm on *Barn Dance,* that makes you my sweetheart, don't it?"

I lifted his arm up like I was picking up a dead rat. "I ain't nobody's sweetheart," I spat, "and I ain't lookin' to be neither." I made a beeline for the women's dressing room.

"Well," he hollered after me, "I reckon that's why they call you Salty. Maybe I'll just go see if I can get some of that sweet stuff your sister's got."

I plopped down on a stool and yanked the ribbons

out of my hair. I was beginning to realize that the male performers I'd idolized on the radio only saw the girl singers as fresh meat. Right then I decided that the only *Barn Dance* cast member I wanted to spend time with was Susan.

And did I ever spend time with Susan! I couldn't see enough of her. She was so smart, so sophisticated —I felt like I knew nothing, and she had everything to teach me. I wanted to soak her up like a sponge.

"I just got a new record in the mail," she'd say. "Why don't you come over and hear it?" I'd sit by the record player, absorbing every note, whether it was Count Basie or Hank Williams.

"You mean to tell me you've not read *Jane Eyre* [or *Of Human Bondage* or *From Here to Eternity*]! Well, for god's sake, borrow it!" I'd borrow whatever book it was, stay up all night reading it, and go back to her the next day, red-eyed but excited and full of questions.

Susan never seemed surprised by the music I had never heard of the books I had never read, but when she found out the extremely limited number of foods I had eaten, she was shocked. "Jesus H. Christ, Glenda! Do you actually expect me to believe that you've never even heard of spaghetti?"

This happened when I was visiting her one afternoon, and she had been telling a story about living in New York and how much spaghetti she and her roommate used to eat because it was so cheap.

I didn't even think before I asked, "What's spaghetti?" Like I told Susan after she was through pitching her little fit, I could just about count on two hands the kinds of food I ate on a regular basis back in Argon: pinto beans, corn bread, fried potatoes, biscuits, gravy, eggs, ham or bacon when we could get it, squirrel when Daddy could shoot it, chicken on Sunday, and greens and corn and tomatoes in the summertime.

Susan looked real sad for some reason. "That's all you've ever had to eat?"

"Well, that and what Mrs. Willard fixes at the boarding house. And there was that omelet you fixed me, and I had a chili dog once at a restaurant in Morgan."

Susan jumped up. "Well, tonight I'm making you spaghetti. You make yourself comfortable, put on a record or something. I'm going to the grocery store."

Susan came back with two bags, one from the grocery store and one from the liquor store. "Needless to say," she said, "you can't get any decent bread in this pathetic excuse for a town, so we'll have to settle for rolls."

She worked in that kitchen like a scientist in her laboratory. Every time she took out an ingredient she thought I might not be familiar with, she'd tell me what it was. "Garlic," she announced, holding up something that looked like the head of a green onion. She pointed to a jar of dried green leaves. "Oregano." I was fascinated. The only seasonings Mama ever used were salt, pepper, and bacon grease.

Spaghetti Night is what I call that night in my memory. It was one of those rare times when you can't remember feeling anything but happy.

Part of the magic was the food itself. That sauce was unlike anything I had ever put in my mouth. The sharp tomato, the pungent garlic, the zesty oregano, the sweet basil — there were so many tastes going on at once that I almost wanted to hold it in my mouth forever. And there was the noodles, and Susan laughing at me when I sucked up the strands that dangled from my mouth. We had wine, too, a deep red that we drank from stemmed glasses that were almost too beautiful and delicate to touch.

But it wasn't just the food itself. It was also that Susan had made something especially for me. And it wasn't just food to fill you up like the corn bread and beans Mama made us in Argon; it was food to be enjoyed. As I looked down at my empty plate, I felt like Susan kept giving and giving to me — like she kept adding the spices to make life exciting and wonderful, instead of just the vale of tears people at home said it was. "Thank you so much," I whispered.

"No need to get all mushy. I just made you a plate of spaghetti, for crissakes," she laughed. "Here, have some more wine."

We talked about all kinds of things that night. She told me she was an only child and her parents hadn't even meant to have her. She told me her mama had pressured her into being a debutante and that she had gotten so drunk on the night of her coming-out party that she tripped over her high heels and fell down the stairs and broke her arm. "The only thing I liked about growing up rich," she said, "was the horses. I always felt free when I was riding my horse. Of course, they made me wear one of those stupid English riding outfits, but in my mind, I was always a cowgirl."

I told her about all the men in Argon working in the mines and how scary it was because you knew if the mine caved in, there'd be nothing anybody could do. I told her how Roy worked in the mines now and Vaughn was about to start to, and how I'd give anything if they'd just go any place but Argon and do anything but mining.

"You're really close to your brothers, aren't you?"

"Oh, yeah. I ran around with them and their buddies the whole time we was growin' up."

"Did you have any close girlfriends?"

"Before you, you mean? Well, there was Angel. She . . . she was the preacher's daughter." I felt myself clamming up. If I told much more, I'd have to tell everything, and I wasn't ready to do that yet. I was too afraid of Susan not liking me. I decided to close the subject, then change it. "But she moved away. Say, you never did tell me about that ring you wear on your pinkie. The only time I've seen you without it is when you're playin' Miz Lucindy."

Susan stared down into her wine glass like there was a bug in the bottom of it. I knew I had said something wrong.

"Lord, I've got a big mouth on me, don't I? Mama always told me my biggest trouble in life was that I didn't know when to hush. Just forget I asked, okay? We'll talk about somethin' else — records or somethin'."

"No, Glenda, I really feel like I should tell you. It's just that . . . I mean, good god, you didn't even know what spaghetti was."

"What does that have to do with anything? I may be ignorant, but I ain't stupid."

"I know you're not stupid, far from it. I'm just afraid —"

"Don't be afraid. I'm your friend, Susan. Nothin' you say is gonna change that."

"Okay, okay, dammit. I'll *try* to explain this anyway. When a woman wears a pinkie ring like this, it means . . . No, wait, let me do this another way." She stuck a cigarette in her mouth and fumbled around with her lighter. I had never seen Susan nervous, and it made me nervous, too. "You remember me talking about Sandra, my roommate in New York?"

"Uh-huh."

"Well, we were more than just roommates."

"You were friends, too, right?"

"Well, yeah, but we were more than that, too. Christ, this is hard. Glenda, Sandra and I were . . . a couple. We kissed each other, we slept in the same bed, we did things sort of like what men and women do. Of course, it's different when it's two women." She stopped for a second, then said, "I've shocked the hell out of you, haven't I? God, I shouldn't have told you. You're just a baby —"

"Angel and me was like that."

"Excuse me?"

"Angel and me was like that. We kissed, we did things in the bed together. I guess I thought we was the only two girls in the world that ever —"

"Now wait just a goddamned minute, Glenda. Do you mean to tell me that out there in the ass-end of nowhere, you were getting naked with the preacher's daughter?"

"Well, it wasn't just about gettin' naked. We loved each other in the spirit of true friendship —"

She hooted with laughter, then leaned over and

wrapped me in a tight bear hug. I hugged her back just as tight. "Oh, Glenda, Glenda, Glenda," she laughed. "You are full of surprises, aren't you?"

When we pulled apart from each other, she grabbed my hand like she didn't want to let go of me all the way. "You still haven't told me what the ring means," I said.

"That's because I had completely forgotten about the damned ring. A pinkie ring on the left hand is a signal to other women-in-the-know that you're a lesbian."

"A what?"

"Here's your second vocabulary lesson for the day. A *lesbian*" — she squeezed my hand —" a *lesbian* is someone like us.

So there's a word for it, I thought. I was repeating in my head, I am a singer; I am a lesbian. It was nice to have two things about me I knew for a fact. I was just thinking this when Susan's lips brushed against mine. It was a short, shy kiss — the length of a heartbeat.

"God, I'm corrupting a minor," she said.

"I was done corrupted before you got ahold of me."

"Then . . . was it okay that I kissed you?"

"Mm-hmm."

"Would it be okay if I did it again?"

"Mm-hmm."

The next kiss was long and slow. She tasted like wine and smoke, and as she pushed me down on my back on the couch, I knew I had been starving to death for this without even knowing it.

Compared to what Susan did to me that night,

what Angel and me had done had just been little girl tea parties. Angel was a girl, but Susan was a woman — a woman who knew exactly what she was doing.

Before I knew it, I was out of my dress and on the floor, and she was on top of me with her thigh between my legs. We were moving, moving, moving until I thought I'd go crazy, and then the whole room was shaking like an earthquake. But the earthquake was coming from me.

I flipped over on my stomach, trying to catch my breath. Susan stroked my hair. "Are you all right? I didn't hurt you, did I?"

"No, ma'am," I laughed. "You didn't hurt me one bit." I turned around to face her. "Now show me what to do."

"What do you mean? Oh — oh! Nothing. You country girls may do it differently, but . . . uh . . . I don't like having that done to me."

"Lord, there'd have to be somethin' wrong with somebody that didn't like that!"

She laughed and kissed me. "No, you see . . . what I like . . . is doing it to you." And so she did.

Afterward, she whispered, "Now you know we can't tell anybody about this, right?"

I thought about Angel's dad. "I know all about that."

"Good. So . . . we probably shouldn't spend the night together."

I couldn't hide how disappointed I was, but I knew she was right. It was spending the night together that got Angel and me into trouble. "Yeah, you're right, I guess. But I hate it."

"I hate it, too. But not nearly as badly as I'd hate it if the *Barn Dance* boys started getting suspicious. So get dressed. I'll drive you home."

As much as I hated to leave, the drive back was beautiful. The old moon had the new moon in its arms just like Susan had held me in her arms. The sky was full of stars, and life was full of possibilities.

Chapter 9

I wonder if I would've gotten tired of working at *Barn Dance* as fast as I did if I hadn't been girlfriends with Susan. I probably would have. I didn't need anybody to tell me I didn't like being grabbed by the band boys or wearing gingham or singing "Down in the Valley" every damn night that *Barn Dance* was performed. Yeah, I would've gotten sick of it anyway, but I think Susan and I really gave each other the courage to leave.

"You're a great singer," Susan would tell me almost every day, "and you deserve to be in charge of your own music instead of singing what that old windbag tells you to sing."

"You're a great actress," I'd tell her, "and you ought to be on Broadway instead of tellin' cornpone jokes on some little ol' radio show." It was like we were feeding each other spoonful after spoonful of courage, so one day we'd both be full enough of it to say, "I quit."

But there was a problem. We couldn't quit. We couldn't quit because Old Tiresome Joe had us under a one-year contract so ironclad that Daniel Webster himself couldn't have argued us out of it. I was committed to one full year at *Barn Dance,* and I had only worked there four months. I had almost decided that Susan and me should just suck it up and work the remaining eight months, but then there was the last straw.

The last straw was, you won't be surprised to know, Emily Cole. One night when we were changing into our costumes in the dressing room, Emily was as happy as she could be, just singing away like a little lark.

"You're in an awful good mood tonight," I said, trying to make conversation.

"I sure am, and you should be, too," she chirped, "because come this Christmas, you won't have me for a sister anymore. How's that for a Christmas present?"

"I don't think I understand."

"Well, I always said I'd just work till I got married, and . . ." She shoved her hand in my face so I could see the diamond engagement ring on her left hand. "Salty, I'm engaged!"

"I wish you wouldn't call me that, Emily." Then, remembering my manners, I said, "But best wishes all the same." Then it occurred to me; she had signed her one-year contract the same time I had signed mine. "But Emily, if you don't mind my askin', how are you gonna get out of your contract?"

She flipped her hair and gave this little sigh like I had just asked the dumbest question she'd ever heard. "But Salty, don't you know? I'm marryin' Lonesome Joe! He's not gonna be lonesome anymore."

My mouth hung open for a second. "But, but Lonesome Joe's gotta be at least forty years older than you!"

"Love knows no age, honey. Love knows no age," she said, like she was much older and wiser than me.

I started to say something mean, but then I thought, *Hey, if she's gone in December, then maybe I can go on as a solo act. And maybe I can be Glenda Mooney instead of half of the Cole Sisters. And maybe —*

Before I could finish my next thought, Emily broke in with, "But don't you worry. Lonesome Joe says he'll bring in a new girl to sing with you, so the Cole Sisters will go on without me."

I was mad as a hornet. Mad because the only way to get out of a contract with *Barn Dance* was to marry Joe Whitcomb. Mad because as long as I stayed at *Barn Dance,* I would never be able to perform as myself. After the show that night, I grabbed Susan by the arm and said, "We have to talk."

She looked startled. "About what?"

"About gettin' the hell out of here."

Our path was clear. We couldn't quit because we couldn't get out of our contracts. We were going to have to get ourselves fired.

Now getting yourself fired from a job isn't the most difficult thing in the world to do. Lord knows, plenty of people have done it. But to get yourself fired on purpose, that takes some imagination and some common sense, too — *imagination* because you might as well go out with some style, and *common sense* because you don't want to do anything that'll get you arrested or shot.

Susan and me talked about lots of ways to do it. Some might've worked, like cussing up a storm on stage. Other things were too wild to even try, like setting the barn on fire. After we finally arrived at what to do, the hard part came. We had to wait till the perfect time to act out our plan.

About a month and a half later, the time came. Emily had a bad cold and wouldn't be able to perform that Saturday night, so I would have to go on by myself. Perfect. On that stage, all by myself, I could do absolutely anything I wanted to.

Well, here's what we did.

That night, Miz Lucindy was scheduled to go on right after the Cole Sisters, so it was a perfect opportunity to act out our plan and get out of there.

Let's just say I didn't go on stage wearing gingham that night. Susan had given me a royal-blue satin gown left over from her debutante days. It was the sexiest dress I'd ever seen, shiny and slinky with rhinestone spaghetti straps. To make it even sexier, I cut it off just above the knee and sewed fringe around the hem, so that when I wiggled, the fringe did, too. I put on that blue dress and some spike-heeled shoes (also from Susan's debutante days). I brushed out my hair, put on some red, red lipstick, and strapped on my guitar. I heard Lonesome Joe's introduction: "Well, I'm afraid that one of our beloved Cole Sisters is a little under the weather, but we do have with us tonight Salty Cole, who just left her dear sister's bedside to come and sing us one of her favorite mountain tunes."

I stifled a giggle and gave him enough time to exit stage left before I came in on the right. When I sashayed out on stage, the audience gasped. I wasn't afraid to do anything. After all, I wasn't performing under my name anyway, and I wanted the final performance of Salty Cole to go down in *Barn Dance* history. I let go with a "da-*da*-da-da-dump" blues riff on the guitar, and as I swayed my hips, the fringe swayed with me. I had planned to sing a Bessie Smith song, but when I was up there, these words that had been floating around in my head just poured out of me:

Well, they say that little girls
Is made of sugar and spice,
But some of us is Salty,
And I think that's twice as nice.
They call me Salty,
Yeah, Salty's what they call me,
So come a little closer,
And see how salty I can be.
Well, Sweetie she is fine
If you like kid stuff,
But for a grown-up, honey,
That just ain't enough —
You need me, Salty,

Salty, that's the truth
'Cause Salty, hon,
Will get rid of that sweet tooth.

They switched the lights off on me, which I figured was a good sign. When the lights came back on, Lonesome Joe said, "I apologize, folks. This is a family program, and you ought not to have had to listen to that. But now here's somebody everybody'll want to listen to, everybody's favorite little gal with all the latest gossip from Possum Creek, Miz Lucindy!"

But what the audience got was not Miz Lucindy, but Susan dressed in flowing white robes. She looked like a queen, and that was who she was playing. She didn't feel like playing Miz Lucindy anymore, so she was playing Medea. She was a great actress. It was funny and sad at the same time to see such a grand performance lost on a confused audience. But like Medea says in her monologue, "If you put new ideas before the eyes of fools, they'll think you foolish and worthless into the bargain." They turned the lights off on her, too, and she ran to join me in the wings.

All of a sudden, I felt an unfriendly hand on my shoulder. I turned around to see Lonesome Joe, who was looking more like Furious Joe. "What the sam hill do you crazy females think you're doin'?" he shouted. "Salty Cole, you're up there dressed like a slut and singin' jungle music. And you, Miz Lucindy, are up there dressed in a bedsheet doin' I don't know what!"

"Medea," Susan said.

"Just cause I said 'I don't know what' don't mean I want to know what!" Lonesome Joe bellowed. He dug in his pocket and threw two bills at us. "Here's the last twenty dollars you'uns is gonna get out of me! I want you to back to your dressin' room and get your things, because you'uns is never comin' on *Barn Dance* property again!" He stomped off, muttering.

Susan and me hugged each other and jumped up and down. We couldn't have been happier. We were fired.

Chapter 10

As soon as we walked into her apartment that night, Susan grabbed a pair of scissors and said, "Follow me to the bathroom, Glenda. I want you to witness this."

"Witness what?"

"The death of Miz Lucindy."

I followed her to the bathroom and watched silently as she started snipping away at her honey-blonde hair. "Are you sure you wanna do this?" I asked.

"Shh, be quiet. This is a funeral." I thought she

might have finally flipped her lid, but I didn't say anything. I just stood there watching the sink fill up with clump after golden clump of Susan's hair.

When she finished, she had a neat little mop of soft, short curls. She picked up the double handful of hair from the sink and dumped it into the trash can. "Good-bye, Miz Lucindy," she called into the trash. "Whew!" she sighed, running her hands up the nape of her neck, then striking a mock dramatic pose, "With God as my witness, I'll never wear pigtails again!"

I laughed, and she reached for my hand. "Come on, kid," she said, grinning. "Let's start the rest of our lives."

And we did. The trouble was, we had spent months planning how to get out of *Barn Dance* and absolutely no time planning what we were going to do with ourselves once we did get out. I felt like I had just been let out of jail. I had the freedom I had dreamed about for months, but I had absolutely no idea what to do with myself now that I could start living life in the present.

We finally decided that I should move out of Mrs. Willard's boarding house and in with Susan. Since we weren't in Lonesome Joe's big, happy family anymore, we didn't care that much about what people thought. Neither of us were that thrilled about staying on in Shady Grove, but the rent there was low, and since we had both gotten ourselves unemployed, we decided to stay there till we made enough money to leave. Then, Susan said, she would take me to live in New York, where she could audition for plays and I could try to get a record deal.

The plan didn't sound as naive to me as it

probably was. As far as I was concerned, every word that came out of Susan's mouth was the wisdom of the ages. And so we sat down to make a list of what each of us had that could be used to make money. The list looked like this:

Susan	Glenda
a car	a voice

Her car and my voice took a lot of abuse the next few months. We must've played every dinky old sweat-smelling, sticky-floored honky-tonk in the state of Kentucky, plus a few in Indiana and Tennessee. Susan would always call the places up first and say, "This is Susan Wilson, the talent agent representing *Shady Grove Barn Dance* singing star Glenda Mooney. Miss Mooney is planning a major tour and was wondering if you might be interested in having her perform at your establishment."

The bar owner would usually say sure, but he could only pay ten dollars or five dollars plus tips or just tips, at which time Susan would say, "Throw in gas money, and you've got yourself a deal." And we'd hit the road.

It's hard to remember those days as anything more than a blur of peanut-butter sandwiches made on the dashboard, body aches from sleeping in the car, and sponge baths in filthy gas-station rest rooms. At night, I'd go to whatever honky-tonk it was, put on this tacky little cowgirl outfit I'd bought in a secondhand store, stand up on a stage behind chicken wire, and sing country songs I'd learned off the car radio.

The chicken wire, in case you don't frequent such establishments, was to protect the singer from the flying beer bottles. At some places, they'd throw bottles at you if they didn't like you, and at others, they'd throw them if they thought you were good. You could never guess what the bottles would mean as you went from place to place, but I always thought throwing them if you didn't like somebody made the most sense. Throwing a beer bottle at a person is a pretty strange way of paying them a compliment.

When I talk about the honky-tonk days, it always sounds awful. But the truth is, I had a real good time. I was with Susan day and night, I was getting to go places I had never been to before, and we were managing to put away a little money so that we might be able to get ourselves to New York one day.

But sometimes there's a bigger plan working than the plans you make for yourself, and that's why Susan and me never got to New York. Of course, the easiest way to explain it is to say it was because of a song I heard on the radio.

We were driving down the road like we did every other day. I was eating my breakfast peanut-butter sandwich, and Susan was smoking a cigarette and playing with the knobs on the radio. She turned past a country station, then past some man preaching, then past this music that shot straight through me like a bolt of lightning. "Liff id theh!" I yelled, my mouth full of peanut butter and stale bread.

"What?"

I swallowed, then said, "Leave it there — on that music!"

"My god, Glenda, I had no idea you liked rock 'n' roll," she said, switching the station back. "It's kid stuff. Jazz and blues are much more —"

"Shh!" I hissed, desperate to hear the music.

Oh, that music. I felt it in my head, my heart, my most private places. My heart pumped and my pulse throbbed to the beat of that drum, and the squealing guitar ripped through me like a sharp sword. It was wild, sexy, dangerous. It was what I wanted to be. The singer's voice purred, snarled, and hiccuped the words, and my arms broke out in goose bumps.

Susan had a point, I guess. The lyrics were real simple — about everybody jumping on "that rock 'n' roll train" — but there was something pure and honest in that simplicity. I had waited sixteen years to hear this song, and when the deejay's voice cut it off, saying, "That was Zagus Peavley, with 'Rock 'n' Roll Train,' " I jumped like I had been awakened from a beautiful dream.

I switched off the radio. "Susan," I said, "you're gonna think I'm crazy, but just don't say anything for five minutes, okay?"

"Fine," she said, lighting a new cigarette off the butt of her old one. "Suit yourself."

I knew she was mad, but I couldn't take the time to do anything about it just then. I tore off part of a brown paper bag that was on the floorboard and grabbed a pen out of the glove compartment. I leaned over the dashboard, and in five minutes, I had written the first song that I ever put down on paper.

"Okay," I said, "you can talk now."

"What the hell has gotten into you, Glenda? You know I can't stand to be shushed."

"I'm sorry I shushed you, honey. But I just wrote a song."

"In five minutes? Prove it."

I reached in the backseat for my guitar. "Only one way to prove it, I reckon." I tuned up. "Now I ain't got the music worked out all the way yet, but this is how it goes." I struck a few chords, then sang,

People say I'm crazy, but I don't care,
'Cause I'm crazy about your wavy hair.
I'm crazy about your ruby lips,
And I'm crazy about your fingertips.

Yeah, I'm crazy, crazy, baby,
Yeah, I'm crazy, crazy, baby.
They say I'm crazy, but it ain't true,
'Cause all I'm crazy 'bout is you!

People say I was crazy from the start,
'Cause all you're gonna do is break my heart.
But they wasn't with us late last night,
When you said you loved me and you held me tight.

I went crazy, crazy, baby,
I go crazy, crazy, baby.
They say I'm crazy, and it must be true,
'Cause, baby, I'm just crazy 'bout you!

I finished and looked at Susan, desperate for her approval. At first, I didn't think I was going to get it, because she crinkled up her forehead at me and said, "You wrote that, just now, in five minutes?"

"Uh-huh."

"No shit?"

"No shit."

She shook her head real fast, like a wet dog, then laughed out loud. "Hot damn, Glenda!" She looked around for other cars, then leaned over and kissed me real quick. Then she laughed again and slapped the steering wheel and honked the horn three times. "Hot damn!" she yelled out the window. "I'm shacked up with a goddamned rock 'n' roll singer! What would my mama say about that?"

Chapter 11

I played "Crazy, Baby" that night at this honky-tonk in Newport, and crazy is exactly how the crowd went. They let loose when I played that song, hollering and dancing on tables and calling out for more. By the third time I played it, I was making up new words and coming up with new guitar licks. I slung off my cowboy hat and let my hair fly free. I danced so hard I had to pull off my boots and play the rest of the set barefoot.

When I came off that stage, I was drunk — drunk with the music and the applause and the dancing. I ran right across the barroom and into Susan's arms. She got real stiff at first — we were always real careful about not being all touchy-feely in public — but she finally gave in and hugged me. "You were incredible up there, Glenda — just amazing."

The bartender, a middle-aged woman wearing too much eye makeup, grinned when she saw us with our arms around each other. "Ain't y'all just as pretty as a picture?" she crowed. "Y'all's sisters, ain't you?"

Susan laughed. "We sure are," she said, giving me a little squeeze.

"I thought you was," the woman said. "Y'all don't look a thing alike, but there was just somethin' about you. I can always tell." She grinned at me. "You done real good up there, honey. How 'bout a beer on the house before we close up?"

One of the fringe benefits of singing at honky-tonks is that people assume that if you're there, you must be old enough to drink. "I'd be much obliged, ma'am," I said. "Can my sister have one, too?"

After we drank our beers, we walked out to the car holding hands. "Do you know where we're going now?" Susan asked as I was loading my guitar into the backseat.

"Back to Shady Grove, I reckon, unless you want to get some sleep first."

"A good guess, but wrong," Susan said with a cigarette clenched between her teeth. "We're going across the river to Cincinnati."

"Cincinnati? How come?"

"Because, my dear, we're going to find a place where you can make a record."

"A record? Susan, ain't nobody gonna want to make a record of me. I ain't ready yet!"

"The woman I heard tonight was most definitely ready to make a record."

"Su-saan," I started to whine.

"Don't Susan me. We need to record this song before you get sick of singing it. There's a little studio in Cincinnati — Lonesome Joe cut a record there once. I can't remember the name of it, but I'd know it if I saw it in the phone book." She turned the key in the ignition and looked at her watch. "Let's see. It's three A.M. now. I bet the studio opens at nine. That'll give us plenty of time to get into town and find out where we're supposed to go. I'll even buy you breakfast. But no dairy products before you sing — just tea with lemon."

She was a force of nature. All I could do was laugh and say, "You're a crazy woman, you know that?"

"You probably shouldn't talk either. Save your voice for the recording session."

We were waiting outside the offices of Honey Lee Records before the doors were opened. Of course, neither of us had had a wink of sleep. Susan was hopped up on coffee and cigarettes and kept pacing back and forth like a jungle cat, muttering, "Goddamn it, don't these people work for a living?" I was just trying to stay awake. I had drunk three cups of tea at the diner where we'd had breakfast, but the caffeine hadn't done me any good. For once, I didn't even feel like singing. I was exhausted and in a strange city, and all I could think about was our bed back in Shady Grove.

Finally, a woman in a tight skirt and high heels came and unlocked the door.

"Ma'am, I'm Susan Wilson," Susan began

enthusiastically, "and I represent the talent of Miss Glenda Mooney. In all my years in show business, I've never seen a performer like Miss Mooney. Why, I firmly believe she is destined to be the biggest female singer since Kitty Wells."

The woman gave us a look that said she had seen it all and didn't give a rat's ass about any of it. "Tell it to the boss man, honey. All I do around here is answer the phones."

The "boss man" didn't get there for another forty-five minutes. Seconds before he got there, I was pleading, "Come on, Susan. I'm dog tired. Let's just go home, okay?"

But then he walked in. Charlie Lee looked like a brick wall with a greasy pompadour on top of it. "Well, well," he boomed. "What a treat to walk into work in the mornin' and be greeted by three lovely ladies!" The secretary rolled her eyes and went back to typing. I smiled the best I could.

Susan went into her routine about how I was going to be bigger than Kitty Wells because I was something really different — a girl rockabilly singer. That was the first time I heard the word *rockabilly*; I liked the sound of it.

"Well, now," Charlie Lee said, grinning. "That is somethin' different — a girl rockabilly singer." He said "girl rockabilly singer" the same way you might say "bearded lady." It was like I was some curiosity of nature. "I don't usually allow auditions without an appointment, but I think I'll make an exception in your case, Miss Mooney. I'm just real curious to hear what a little ol' gal like you can do with a rock 'n' roll song."

It was the perfect thing for him to say because it

made me mad, and when I'm mad, I play *good.* We went back into the sound booth, and before he even knew what hit him, I tore into "Crazy, Baby." My voice hiccupped and moaned and did things I didn't even know it could do. I wanted to show Mr. Charlie Lee a thing or two about what a "gal" could do with a rock 'n' roll song.

When I finished, he said, "That's a fine little tune, Miss Mooney. Who wrote it?"

"I did."

"You did?" He slapped his leg, laughing. "Well, I'll be dogged! I reckon you do see somethin' new every day. Let me tell you the way we do things at Honey Lee Records, darlin'. You sign a contract with us for one record — an *A* side and a *B* side. We pay for production costs, and we'll get the record out in stores. For that, we get two cents off every record sold, plus the rights to publish the music. Now you've got to promote the record your own self, and that means drivin' all over creation and beggin' deejays to play it."

I heard every word he said, but I was having a hard time taking it all in. "You mean . . . you're offering me a contract?"

He laughed. "It sounds that way, don't it? Now there's just one thing about that little song of yours, honey. Didn't you sing a part that said somethin' like, 'I'm crazy about your ruby lips?' "

"Yessir." I had no idea what he was getting at.

"Well, I reckon you just made a little mistake writin' that part, 'cause boys don't have ruby lips, do they?"

"I guess not." I couldn't exactly tell him that Susan had ruby lips and the song was about her.

"I mean a boy might have ruby lips if he was wearin' lipstick or somethin', but then he'd be a sissy boy, and you wouldn't be singin' no love songs to a sissy boy, would you?"

"No, sir." I wouldn't be singing love songs to any boy.

"Well," he said, grinning, "you just sing it 'tender' lips instead, and that ought to take care of it. Now I'm gonna go see if I can round you up a drummer and a bass fiddle player, and I'll get Miss Carter to type up your contract."

"Okay," I said. I was too excited to let the "ruby lips" thing bother me. People were going to be able to walk into a store and buy the new Glenda Mooney record. Kids in drugstores would be dancing to "Crazy, Baby."

"In the meantime," he said, "you and your agent there can be talkin' about what you wanna sing for your *B* side."

As soon as he was out of sight, I kissed Susan right on her ruby lips. "I told you you were ready," she said. "I'm so proud of you."

"I love you so much, Susan," I said. "Thank you for making me do this." Then panic hit me. "Oh lord, what am I gonna do for my *B* side? I don't have two songs."

"You've got that song you did your last night on *Barn Dance.*"

"Yeah, but that was just a joke. I wouldn't want to put it on a record or nothin'."

"Oh, for god's sake, Glenda, it's just a *B* side; nobody's gonna listen to it. You can sing any old piece of shit you want. Just sing something you know really well, and don't worry about it."

"Of course." The choice was obvious.

"Crazy, Baby" backed with "Down in the Valley" was recorded that afternoon in five takes. None of the screwups were my fault, either. The drummer and the bass fiddle player needed a couple of takes to get "Crazy, Baby" down, and once a piece of recording equipment messed up. Honey Lee Records was a real shoestring operation. Of course, I didn't know that at the time.

After the record was pressed, Susan and me set to promoting up a storm. She went to her daddy and told him she was having female trouble and embarrassed him into giving her some money for medical expenses. She came home with two hundred dollars. I was real mad when she told me what she'd done. "Susan, you told me you was gonna ask him for a loan. Lyin' to your daddy ain't right — particularly not about that. You'll worry him to death, makin' him think you have female trouble."

She laughed. "I do have female trouble. The female I live with needs money to travel to promote her record."

"Well, I just don't feel right about you borryin' your daddy's money on my account."

"Oh, don't worry so much, Glenda. He's loaded. He won't miss a couple hundred bucks. Besides, borrowing this money was in my best interest, too. The more we promote this record, the more money you'll make off it. And the more money you make, the sooner we can be in New York and I can start auditioning for plays."

We took Mr. Wilson's money and traveled all over the Southeast with it. The trunk of the car was full of records, and whenever we passed a town that looked big enough to have a radio station, we stopped by to chat with the disc jockey and give him a free record. We sweet-talked every deejay from Kentucky to Florida, smiling till our lips bled, even at the mean ones. By the end of the day, we were always so wore out from sweet talking that we couldn't even be nice to each other.

Of course, we couldn't travel to every radio station in the country on two hundred dollars, so the places that were too far away to go to, we sent free records and sexy pictures of me. The sexy picture was Susan's idea; I wasn't that crazy about it myself. When I had protested, she said, "You're the most beautiful girl in the world, Glenda, and if showing how pretty you are helps get you what you want, I think you should do it."

I looked down at my slinky green sheath dress. It had a split in the skirt, which, as far as I could tell, didn't do anything but show off how skinny my legs were. "The most beautiful girl in the world, my ass!" I looked down at my lack of cleavage. "What about Jane Russell?"

Susan didn't bat an eye. "You're ten times more beautiful than Jane Russell."

How could I resist her? I put one high heel up on a chair, balanced my guitar on my thigh, turned toward the camera, and smiled.

"Of course, the thing is," Susan said after she snapped the picture, "all those radio men will only get to look at you." She took the guitar from me and put her hands around my waist. "I'm the only one who gets to touch." My slinky dress didn't stay on long after that.

I didn't realize how much airplay "Crazy, Baby"

was getting until the gig I played at the Grover County Agricultural and Industrial Fair. It was my most impressive gig so far. I was opening for Jimmy Everett, who was a fairly big country act with a couple of top-twenty hits.

I was getting ready to go on stage when Jimmy Everett's steel guitar player tapped me on the shoulder. "Congratulations, kiddo," he said.

"Thanks," I said distractedly. "What for?"

"For bustin' the charts, that's what for!"

I couldn't have been any dumber if I'd been poleaxed. "Huh? What charts?"

His eyes got big. "Jesus, you don't know, do you? Hey, Virgil!" he hollered. "Bring that *Billboard* magazine out here, will you?"

I looked down at the list in the magazine he was holding. "Crazy, Baby" by Glenda Mooney. Number 46. "Susan! Susan!" I screamed.

She came running out of the dressing room like Boris Karloff or somebody was chasing her. "Glenda, what is it? What's wrong?"

I handed her the magazine and pointed dumbly at Number 46. "Oh my god!" she screamed. "Oh my fucking god!"

I hugged Susan. I hugged the boy in Jimmy Everett's band who I didn't even know, and all the time, Susan kept saying, "Oh my god. Oh my fucking god."

The boy looked at her, then at me. "She's sure got a dirty mouth on her, don't she?"

I laughed. "She sure does," I said.

I played one of the best shows ever that night. By that time, I was developing what fancy people might call a repertoire. I'd written two songs besides "Crazy,

Baby" — a slow number called "Leaving Me Blue" and a dance tune, "Shake It Loose." The three songs I'd written, plus two or three standards I added my own twist to, made for a solid opening act. Even the people who were definitely there to see Jimmy Everett instead of me seemed to have a good time.

After the show, Susan and me walked around the fair. I felt like a little kid, except I'd never gotten to go anyplace that fun when I actually was a little kid. I ate a candy apple and two sticks of cotton candy. It's a wonder I didn't make myself sick, but right then, life was so sweet I just couldn't get enough sweetness in me.

We sat in our cart at the top of the Ferris wheel. The lights below us glowed in blurry reds, greens, and yellows. The calliope was playing a happy tune. I was seventeen years old, I was in love, and I had a record on the *Billboard* charts. I squeezed Susan's hand and rested my head on her shoulder. "It don't get better than this, darlin'. It just don't get better than this."

Chapter 12

Once you've got a song on the charts, even if it's real low on the charts, your phone starts ringing. It was about eleven o'clock in the morning when I got the phone call that thereafter was simply called *the* phone call. Susan and me hadn't gotten in from our gig til about three A.M., so we were still snoring away. And even though I cleared my throat before I picked up the phone, my hello still came out as a croak.

"I'm lookin' for a Glenda Mooney," a man's voice said.

Now maybe it's just because of the way I was brought up, but when I hear about strangers looking for me, I always assume I'm in trouble, so I swallowed real hard before I said, "Speaking."

"Well, Miz Mooney, you sure are a hard little old gal to find! This here's Big Bert Riley at Venus Studios over in Nashville. I caught your act at that little fair you played over in Martinsboro, and you plumb got away before I could tell you how good you was."

"Uh . . . well, thank you for callin' to tell me."

"Honey, I wouldn't have spent all this time trackin' you down if all I wanted to do was tell you you're good. I figure you know that already. Am I right?"

I laughed. "I guess so."

"Well, Glenda, what I want to talk to you about is fame and money. You like fame and money, don'tcha?"

"Well, I reckon I need to get me a little more of both before I give you a real answer, sir."

That made him laugh. "Well, that's what I wanna do for you, Glenda. Venus is a real successful studio, Glenda. We handle Tommy Kain and Jimmy Hart and many more besides. We want the world to know that Memphis ain't the only town in Tennessee that can rock 'n' roll. You know what I'm sayin'?"

"I think so." I hoped I did.

"Well, the thing is, Glenda, we ain't got one single girl rockabilly singer on our label, and with your help, I think we could change that. We're a real studio, not like that little hole in the wall in Cincinnati you made your first record at. We're talkin' real fame and real money here. What do you say?"

I didn't know to ask any questions except "When can I start?"

"Well, the way I see it," he said, "you can start just as soon as you get that hot little voice of yours down to Nashville."

We were packed, out of the apartment, and on the road by two o'clock that afternoon. Susan was as excited as I was. When we drove past *Shady Grove Barn Dance,* she reached out the window with her middle finger stuck up in the air.

"Susan, stop that! Somebody'll see you."

"Who cares? You plan on coming back to this hellhole any time soon?"

She was right. I gave *Barn Dance* the finger, too.

The funny thing was that by driving from Shady Grove in the direction of Nashville, we were also driving toward Argon. This made me feel strange, like I was going back in time to when I was just a pesky little old girl hanging onto Roy and Vaughn. All of a sudden I felt homesick. Nashville was a long way past Argon, and who knew when I'd get back to see my family. Besides, I wanted Susan to see Argon — the little house where I grew up, the river where I nearly got myself killed, the woods where I decided to devote my life to music. Susan would never really know me unless she saw the place I came from.

"Susan, Argon's just a little ways down the road. I was wonderin' if maybe we could stop there for an hour or so."

She squinted at me through cigarette smoke. "What for?"

"Oh, I don't know. I just ain't seen my mama in a long time. Or Roy and Vaughn."

"Oh, I get it," Susan said. "Now that you're going to be all rich and famous, you don't want to forget your humble origins."

I grinned a little. "Yeah, maybe that's it." But it wasn't really. I wasn't even sure I understood what she meant. Seems like a person would have to be hit on the head not to remember where they came from.

Argon looked the same. I hadn't been gone that long. But somehow I got the feeling that if I had been gone for twenty years, it would still look the same — the same chipped paint on the buildings, the same coal dust everywhere. If I had stayed here, I wondered, would I have stayed the same, too?

"Is this it?" Susan asked.

"This is it."

"There's not much to it, is there?"

"Guess not."

"Where are we going?"

"Over to see Mama, I reckon."

"Shouldn't we call her first?"

"How come?"

"Well, you know, to see if she's home."

I laughed. Where else would Mama be?

Susan kind of sucked in her breath when she saw the house. It did look kind of rough, I reckon. The roof needed fixing, and the paint had wore off it. There wasn't really any grass around the house, either — just some dirt for the chickens to scratch in. "Glenda," she said, "this is never how I pictured it. I kind of thought of a farmhouse with a barn —"

"Now what in blue blazes would a coal miner want with a barn?" She just kept sitting there, so finally I said, "Are you gettin' out of the car or not?"

"Oh. Yeah. Sorry." She got out, but she made sure to follow several steps behind me.

I opened the screen door and walked in. She was standing over the stove, like always. "Mama?" I called.

She didn't jump or anything. She just turned around real calm and said, "Glenda. Lord, girl, what have you done to your hair?"

"Just trimmed it and curled it a little is all. Mama, this is my friend, Susan."

Susan smiled at her, gearing up her "nice girl" routine. "A pleasure to meet you, Mrs. Mooney."

Mama squinted at Susan briefly, then turned back to the stove. "Well, I reckon I orta peel some more taters then."

Susan kept right on trying to be charming. "We're moving to Nashville, Mrs. Mooney. Glenda has a big, fat recording contract waiting for her down there. She's going to be the biggest girl singer since Kitty Wells."

"That a fact?" Mama said dully. She looked even tireder than I'd remembered her. "Well, I reckon your daddy'll be home soon. The mines is fixin' to let out."

"How's Daddy doin'?"

" 'Bout the same, I reckon. You know your daddy. He's kindly aggravated at Roy right now, but he won't say nothin' about it."

"Why's he mad at Roy?" Daddy had never showed

any feelings to us kids one way or the other, so I was kind of surprised he had it in him to get mad at one of us.

"Aah, Roy's fixin' to quit the mines. He's got this little girl he's wantin' to marry, and she's talked him into takin' a job down in Georgia. Can't say I care much for her nor her big ideas neither. Vaughn's stickin' right by his daddy, though."

"Well, that's good, I reckon." Actually, I was glad Roy was quitting the mines, but I wasn't surprised that Daddy was mad about it. Daddy was a company man, always had been.

I could tell Susan had no idea how to act. She sat in a beat-up old chair with her ankles crossed like she was at some kind of society ladies' tea party. The awkwardness didn't ease up any when Daddy and Vaughn walked in.

I was used to the way they looked when they got home from the mines, black from head to toe except for the whites of their eyes and the pink of their lips. Susan just sat there with her mouth hanging open.

"Well, Glenda," Vaughn said, "good to see you. Your friend there's lookin' at us like we're about to put on a minstrel show."

"Vaughn, this is Susan," I said.

"Pardon me if I don't shake your hand, Vaughn. I've heard a lot about you."

"Well, I hope I'll get time to set the record straight." He grinned, his teeth yellow against the black coal dust. "Say, maybe I'll just not warsh this here coal off. Maybe I'll just sit here lookin' at them pretty blue eyes of yourn till I turn into a diamond!"

"Son, stop runnin' your mouth and go warsh,"

Daddy said. "Ever since his brother found him a gal, all Vaughn's thought about is gettin' him one, too."

"It's good to see you, Daddy," I said.

He looked down at the floor. "Well," he said, then nodded his head at me and Susan. "Reckon I orta go get warshed up my own self."

Supper started out awkward and ended up awful. Supper itself was probably what eighty-five percent of my meals had been growing up: pinto beans, corn bread, fried potatoes, and buttermilk to drink. Mama, Daddy, Vaughn, and me all picked up our slabs of corn bread and crumbled them up in our beans. Susan buttered hers and nibbled on it. I could tell she didn't like the food. She took a bite here and there, but mostly she just pushed it around on her plate to make it look like there was less of it. Mama saw her and wasn't fooled.

To make things worse, Vaughn kept talking to Susan, trying to be all charming, which, as much as I loved him, made me want to kick him under the table. "Where's your people from?" he asked her.

"My mother and father are both Scotch-Irish, so I guess Scotland and Ireland."

Vaughn grinned. "You ain't got no accent."

"Oh," Susan said, finally getting his meaning. "You were asking me where *I'm* from. Lexington, Kentucky."

But I couldn't keep up with Vaughn and Susan's conversation because Mama kept wanting to talk to me about Jesus. Some time after I'd left, she had found the Lord again, and I'd have just as soon she'd left him where she'd found him. Sitting over on a stand in the corner she had a Bible so big you could've beat a cow to death with it.

"You go to church over there in Shady Grove, Glenda Fay?"

"Sometimes," I lied. "When I have time."

"Well, you should always make time for the Lord."

"Yes, Mama."

Daddy just stared at his plate. If he had any feelings about Vaughn's flirting or Mama's preaching, he kept them to himself. He just ate methodically, like a bull chewing its cud.

"Well, actually, what I really am is an actress," I heard Susan say to Vaughn.

Mama heard her, too. "I used to want to be an actress," she said. Everybody but Daddy looked up at her, surprised. "I used to go to the show and read movie magazines and such as that. But there comes a time in a gal's life when she has to give up her silly notions and get married and have babies and get right with God."

Susan, for once, was speechless. Lucky for her, she didn't have to say anything because Roy busted in right then. Well, it would've been lucky if it hadn't opened up a whole new can of worms.

"Sissy!" Roy said. Beside him was a little slip of a girl with big brown eyes and curly black hair. "We was just out walkin' and seen that big fine car out there and wondered who it belonged to. That yours, Sissy?"

"No." I nodded in Susan's direction. "It's hers."

"Aw, I thought you might've bought it with the money you made offa that record. They got it on the jukebox in the drugstore over in Morgan. We was in there the other day, and I put it on, and told everbody in there that that was my baby sister singin'."

The girl smiled. "Like to embarrassed me to death."

Roy gave her a little squeeze. I could tell he was crazy about her. "This here's Delia. We're fixin' to get married and move down to Georgia."

"That's what Mama said."

"Yeah, I got me a job at the big textile mill down in Lynnville. I keep tellin' Vaughn and Daddy there ain't no future in the mines. They've already started layin' off boys here, makin' the operation smaller. I figure I orta get on out before they kick me out. I tell Vaughn he orta do the same, but he won't listen to me. Will you, Vaughn?"

Vaughn looked up at Roy with genuine rage in his eyes. "Lord, Roy, can't I even eat my supper without you goin' on about this? If you wanna go down to Georgia and make washrags, that's your business. But me and Daddy, we're miners. Ain't we, Daddy?"

I saw Delia give Roy a pleading look. "Sorry to disturb your supper, folks," Roy said, like he was talking to a roomful of strangers. "I reckon we orta be headin' on. Good to see you, Glenda."

"Nice to meet you, Delia," I said, feeling like I had to say something nice to the poor girl. She probably couldn't wait to get to Georgia to get away from my family.

Me and Susan didn't hang around long after we finished eating. We were a long way from Nashville and couldn't get there soon enough.

Mama followed us out on the porch. She put her hand on my cheek and said, "I worry about you, Glenda Fay."

"I know, Mama." When I got in the car, there were tears in my eyes.

"Well, that was a barrel of laughs," Susan said as she started the car.

"What do you mean?"

"Oh, nothing. It just looks like your parents would be a little bit proud of you . . . or glad to see you . . . or something."

"They were glad to see me."

"Jesus, what do they do if they're not glad to see you? Shoot you on sight?"

"No, it's . . . oh, I don't know. It's hard to explain. You're just not used to mountain people."

"I guess not. Where I come from, the corners of people's mouths turn up when they're glad to see you."

"Well, I don't see you goin' home to your perfect family that often."

"My parents aren't perfect. As a matter of fact, they're perfect assholes. It's just that they . . . they have some manners."

I was getting real mad. "Well, I'm sorry we don't all have your charm school education. It's just that charm don't enter into the picture that much when you're busy worryin' about where your next meal is comin' from."

Susan sighed. "I'm sorry. It was just strange for me is all. I don't mean to sound like some spoiled little rich girl. And your brothers are very nice."

"Oh, yeah, Vaughn was real nice, wasn't he?

Makin' eyes at each other while you told him all your big tales about bein' a AC-tress!"

I knew Susan was mad because she was driving way too fast. "Now, Glenda, that's absolutely ridiculous, and you know it! You know I don't like boys."

I did know that Susan didn't like boys, but I didn't care. I felt mean-spirited, like picking a fight, and so I was. "Well, that didn't seem to stop you from tryin' to impress him. You love a good audience, don't you? Somebody who'll sit all googly-eyed and say, 'Did you really do that, Susan? Did you really say that? Oh, Susan, you're sooo sophisticated. Oh, Susan, you're sooo interestin'. You don't really need to be with a person, Susan. Your perfect match would be a great big ear!"

When she turned to look at me, a tear was running down her cheek. It was the first time I'd ever seen her cry. "I remember when you loved my stories," she whispered.

I felt terrible. "I'm sorry. I still love your stories. It's just . . . well, if I was a boy and brung you home, Vaughn'd know to stay the hell away from you."

Susan wiped her face. "Life's complicated, isn't it?" She lit a cigarette. "Jesus Christ, how could he be so blind? I'm a great big bull dyke!"

We both started laughing — the kind of laughter that soothes frazzled nerves. When we were quiet again, I said, "Susan, what's a bull dyke?"

She laughed so hard she had to pull off to the side of the road.

Chapter 13

"Now you gotta be careful," Big Bert said as soon as Susan and me sat down in the Venus Records' office. "Just 'cause you're a rock 'n' roll singer, that don't mean you ain't a respectable young lady. Don't get me wrong. We want you to look pretty when you perform, but we don't want you to look cheap or vulgar. Teenage girls all over the country are gonna wanna be just like you, and we don't want that to be a cause for worry for their parents. Do you see what I'm sayin'?"

"Yessir," I said, eyeing the gold records that were plastered all over the walls.

"Good. So you can wiggle around on stage a little bit, but don't make any moves that might be, you know . . . suggestive."

"You mean I can't dance like Zagus Peavley does?"

"Lord, no. Pretty young girl shakin' her behind like that, it'd start a riot." He puffed on his cigar. "And as far as what you wear goes . . . how old are you, Glenda?"

"Eighteen."

"Right, so you're a teenager. So dress like one. I've seen pictures of you in those slinky dresses, and frankly, I think they're a little too old for you. There's nothin' wrong with wearin' sweaters and skirts or even blue jeans and saddle shoes up on stage. It's what most of the girls in the audience'll be wearin', and it won't put the wrong kind of ideas in people's heads, you know?"

"Yessir." I didn't want to look like some silly teenybopper; I wanted to look like a diva. But I wanted that Venus Records deal so bad I would've performed wearing a feed sack if Big Bert had asked me to.

He turned to Susan. "And what do you do?"

"I'm her manager."

He laughed. "Well, honey, you've just managed yourself out of a job. As long as Glenda's under contract here, I'll be taking care of her career." He flashed me a grin. "Ready to make a record?"

I recorded "Shake It Loose" backed with "Leaving Me Blue." Big Bert had found me a couple of real professional musicians, a stand-up bass player and a drummer. We sounded great. It was too bad Susan wasn't there to hear it. Big Bert wouldn't let her into the sound booth.

Looking back on it, I guess Susan got shut out of things from the first day we hit Nashville, and I was just too excited by my career to notice. Nashville was definitely the place for me to make it in the music business, but there wasn't any way Susan could build her acting career there. And now that I was coming into my own, I didn't hang on to Susan's every word like I used to. Her acting dreams were frozen, and I wasn't her perfect, adoring little pupil anymore.

The inevitable happened one night after we'd been living in Nashville for about two months. We'd been traveling in different circles for a while. Susan didn't like to hang out with my musician friends; she said she'd gotten her fill of the band boys back in Shady Grove. She started going at night alone, dressed in slacks and button-down shirts. When I'd beg to go with her, she'd say, "Go play with your guitar pickers, Glenda. You're famous now. You can't be seen where I'm going." So we'd go our separate ways and meet each other in bed about two in the morning.

Except for that one night. I'd been out at a bar where the Opry people hung out after the show, and I got back to the apartment about one-fifteen. As I turned the key in the door, I heard Bessie Smith on the record player. I walked in to see Susan curled up on the couch with a chestnut-haired girl in high heels and a flowered dress. She could've been even younger than me from the looks of her, and she was looking at Susan like she was the eighth wonder of the world.

As soon as Susan saw me, she tried to let on that nothing was happening. "Glenda," she said, plastering a big fake smile on her face. "This is Dixie."

Even if she had been a good enough actress to pull off the casual bit, I would've known what was going on by the fear in Dixie's eyes. At first I wanted to pounce on the girl, to drag her into a hair-pulling fight to the death, but then I realized it wasn't her fault. She had no way of knowing that Susan had a girlfriend. "Dixie," I said, my voice shaking, "it's awful late. Hadn't you best be gettin' on home?"

As soon as she was out of the door — and believe me, it was soon — I turned to Susan and said in a surprisingly calm voice, "That's it."

She looked at me like I was talking something other than English. "What?"

"That's it. It's over."

"It?"

"Us."

"Don't I get a chance to explain?"

"There ain't nothin' to explain. I've got eyes. I know what I seen."

"Glenda —"

"Dixie, huh? Well, I reckon you've found you somebody even trashier than me. I bet you've just got *loads* of stuff to teach her. Well, I hope you enjoy your new little student 'cause I just graduated."

She was pacing back and forth like a wild animal. "You can't just leave me like this, Glenda. You've dragged me to a strange city —"

"You don't seem to be havin' much trouble makin' friends."

"I don't have a job; I've got no place to live."

"Look, you can have the goddamned apartment. The rent's paid up for the next two months, even. That'll give you time to decide what you're gonna do. The fact that I'm even makin' this offer probably means that I either have a halo over my head or that I'm the stupidest person that ever lived. Just let me sleep on the couch tonight. I'll be out in the morning."

I didn't have to give Susan the apartment, and I probably only did it because I felt bad for not paying more attention to her. Sometimes I still wonder if the scene with Dixie happened because Susan wanted to get caught.

I never got a chance to look for a new apartment that morning because Big Bert called me at seven o'clock. "Look, Glenda," he said, "I'm sorry to call you so early, but when you find out what I'm calling about, I don't think you'll be sore at me."

"What is it?" I had cried myself to sleep on a hard couch just four hours before, and my tongue felt like a dry sponge.

"Jimmy Lee Sizemore has had to drop out of the Venus-sponsored tour he was on with Tommy Kain and Octavius Richey. He collapsed on stage from nervous exhaustion. That's what we're callin' it anyway. It was really more like a drunken stupor. Ol' Jimmy Lee's been hittin' the sauce too heavy to hold up his end of the bargain, so we need somebody to replace him on the tour. And I figure you've got a new record to promote, so —"

"You're askin' me to go on tour with Tommy Kain and Octavius Richey?"

"That's right. The catch is — well, I'm askin' you

to do it now. The tour hits Memphis tomorrow night, and somebody needs to be in Jimmy Lee's spot."

I packed my suitcase the second I hung up the phone. I was out of the apartment before Susan even woke up.

Chapter 14

Octavius Richey was the first black man I ever met. Now don't look at me like I've got on a white hood and robe. Think about it. This was 1957 when segregation was going strong, and I was a little ol' girl from the middle of nowhere in Kentucky. I had seen black people before, of course, like that time in the woods in Argon, but Octavius Richey was the first black person who would become my friend.

That first day on the tour bus bound for Memphis, I just sat there like I'd been hit in the head. Everything was moving so fast. In the course of eight hours, I had left my girlfriend, packed up all my belongings, and loaded them on this bus full of strangers, which was the closest thing I had to a home. I couldn't even get excited about being on a big concert tour. Every time I tried to get myself juiced up about it, I saw Dixie's big blue eyes looking at Susan worshipfully — the way I used to look at her.

"Whatsa matter, girlie girl? You too good to talk to the likes of Mr. Kain and me?"

I looked up to see a willowy man in a pink jacket, pink pants, and a charcoal-gray silk shirt. He was probably just about six feet tall, but his pompadour added a good five inches to his height. It was the most incredible hair I'd ever seen. Shiny and black, it rose up from his head like a steeple on a church. His skin was the color of coffee with just a few drops of cream, and when he smiled, I saw that his right front tooth was made out of gold. From the way he looked, I wouldn't have been surprised if he had been born with it.

"Oh, I'm sorry," I said. "I didn't mean to be unfriendly. I just got in real late last night, and Big Bert called me at seven this mornin'."

"Spent all night howling with the dogs and had to get up with the chickens, huh?"

"That's about the size of it."

"Well, that's all right. I just wanted to make sure you wasn't stuck up or nothin'. Some white folks get funny, you know, around colored people."

"Oh, lord, no, that's not it. I'm sorry —"

"Oh, look at you blush!" he squealed, laughing.

"Now you're colored, too, except you're red." He threw his head back, cackling. "Ooh, I just love to make the white folks squirm!"

"Now you stop pickin' on that li'l ol' girl," a voice drawled from over his shoulder. It was Tommy Kain, who was as little and scrawny as a banty rooster and twice as proud. He was drinking from a flask and smoking a cigarette. "It's a pleasure to have a lady on board," he said, wiping the mouth of his flask on his shirttail and offering me a drink.

Octavius poked Tommy in the ribs. "You can tell he's a gentleman 'cause he wipes the slobber off his bottle before he offers you a drink. On his shirttail, no less!"

I turned up the flask and took three big swallows. I needed it. It had been a hell of a night.

"Look at that girl drink!" Octavius hollered. "We're gonna have some fun on this trip, let me tell you!"

We did, too. We'd put on a rocking show, then stay up half the night drinking and playing our guitars. It was only in the early hours of the morning, alone in my hotel room, when I'd cry for Susan.

Honey, you could fill up a book with stories about Tommy and Octavius. Tommy was a bigger mess of contradictions than anybody else I ever met. He was a gentleman, but a rascal. He was a poor white Mississippian, but he wasn't racist. He said he had spent too much time picking cotton for that. And secrets — he was full of them.

One night I was in his room. Octavius had one of his sick headaches and had called it a night early, and Jeb the stand-up bass player and Les the drummer had gone out with a couple of girls who'd come to see them backstage, so Tommy and me were all alone, drinking bourbon straight out of the bottle. We had been comparing coal mining in Kentucky with sharecropping in Mississippi when all of a sudden he turned to me and said, "You got a boyfriend, Glenda?"

My stomach knotted up. I had come to love Tommy like I loved my brothers. I didn't want him making a move and messing things up. "Well, no, but —"

"That's too bad. You oughta get you one," he said, like I could go down to the corner store and buy me a boyfriend. "You're a beautiful girl, Glenda. I was just thinkin' I'd ask you to spend the night with me, except seein' as how I'm married, I ought not to be doin' that."

"Tommy, you're *married*?" He had never said a word about it.

He looked at me real serious, real drunk but real serious. "Glenda, you've gotta promise not to tell nobody. Nobody knows about it, not even Octavius or Big Bert."

"I promise. But why is it such a big secret?" I understood why I had to keep my mouth shut about my love life, but why should Tommy?

"It just wouldn't be good is all. She's this little girl from back home, still lives with her mama and daddy. They don't even know we're married. She ain't but fourteen years old."

I didn't say anything. Back in the mountains, that kind of thing went on all the time. "Well, you're probably smart not to tell anybody yet."

"I love her, though, Glenda. I love her with my

whole heart." He reached into his pocket and pulled out his wallet. "Here's her picture. Ain't she the prettiest thing you ever seen?"

It was a school picture of a gawky, coltish fourteen-year-old girl. "She sure is," I said. "Now you take good care of her, Tommy," I said, thinking of Susan and me. "Don't you ever hurt her."

"Oh, no, Glenda," he said earnestly. "I never would."

Another time we were in Cincinnati, and Tommy and me had gone inside this deli to get sandwiches for the road. Octavius, of course, had to wait in the bus, and so Jeb and Les were keeping him company. The kinds of sandwiches they had were posted on the wall, and I went ahead and ordered for Octavius, Jeb, Les, and me. When I turned to ask Tommy what he wanted, he was staring at his shoes like he was all embarrassed. "Uh . . . they got ham sandwiches?" he asked. Right in front of him, big as life, was a sign that said HAM SANDWICH, 35 CENTS.

It clicked in my head for the first time. Tommy couldn't read. He could write the greatest rockabilly songs in the world, but he did it in his head, not on paper. I never told him I knew this secret, but from then on, I always ordered for him in restaurants and made a point of reading important signs aloud. It was an unspoken agreement. I wouldn't say anything about him not being able to read, but I would save him from some of the embarrassment it caused him.

Of course, Octavius and me had our own unspoken agreement. I was about ninety-five percent sure he was as queer as a three-dollar bill, and I knew he thought the same about me. With him, it was pretty obvious. In 1957, most men were wearing gray flannel suits. No straight man would've been as flashy as Octavius, coming on stage in a pink satin suit and a dyed-to-match pink mink cape. Straight men who wanted to rebel in 1957 did it by looking tough, not glamorous.

I think he figured me out because I never said a word about my romantic life. I'd talk about my childhood, my family, my music, other people's music, but no boyfriends' names ever came up. After a while, he had to get suspicious. I had to be writing those sexy songs to somebody.

Our moment of truth came one night after a nasty scene in Chattanooga. We were playing a show at the auditorium at eight, so around six-thirty, Tommy, Jeb, Les, me, and Octavius went to check the place out and get our equipment set up. The security guard just nodded at the first four of us when we walked in the front door, but when Octavius tried to pass him, he grabbed his jacket sleeve.

"Excuse you, sir," Octavius said. "Do you know how much I paid for this suit?"

"Now, look, I don't want no trouble here," the guard said nervously. "But if you're making a delivery, you need to use the back door."

"The only thing I'm delivering," Octavius huffed, "is my talent to this stage."

"Uh . . ." The guard was obviously confused.

"He's performing here tonight," I broke in. "He's Octavius Richey."

The guard squinted. "He don't look like Octavius Richey."

"Well, who do I look like to you? Miss Bessie Smith?"

"Just show him some ID, Octavius," I said.

Mumbling under his breath, he fished his wallet out of his purple pants. "Here," he said, holding a card out to the man.

"Oh . . . oh, well, I sure am sorry. I've heard you on the radio, and you just never sounded like . . . uh, well . . . colored."

"Lord help me, I've done turned into Pat Boone!" Octavius snatched his card back from the guard and marched past him.

The guard turned to me and said, "Your friend there needs to learn him some respect."

"That's funny, I was just about to say the same thing to you."

Octavius put on a great show that night, but afterward, I could tell the thing at the door had really gotten to him. When Tommy said, "I'm buyin' the beer for the party tonight, Okie" — he always called Octavius Okie on the grounds that Octavius was just too much work to say — Octavius said, "Oh, there ain't gonna be a party for me tonight, hon. I been looking a little rugged lately from the hard living and all. I better catch up on my beauty rest."

I hung out with Tommy in his room for a while, but then I grabbed two beers and went to look in on Octavius.

I banged on the door of the bus until Octavius opened it. He was wearing purple silk pajamas. "If you're moving the party here, then it had better be a slumber party," he said.

"I thought you might like a beer to go to sleep on."

"I prefer a pillow myself."

"I oughta smack you for that one. Can I come in for a minute?"

"Oh, I guess so, if you're gonna stand there looking all big-eyed at me like some starving mountain child. Sit on my cot if you want. We can have a real slumber party, girl talk and everything."

After I sat down and sipped my beer a minute, I said, "I just wanted to say I really hated what happened at the door tonight. I know things like that go on all the time — worse things, too — but this was the first time I had to see it."

"Maybe it was just the first time you noticed it."

"Maybe. And it was extra bad because, well, you're my friend."

"You're a sweet girl, Glenda." He patted my arm. "Well, I'd be lying if I said it didn't bother me. The inconveniences I can put up with — sleeping in the bus, peeing in a Mason jar when there's not a colored bathroom to be found, washing in the bucket of hot water you bring me every morning. But things like that business at the door tonight make me mad enough to spit nails. Still and all, though, I'm pretty lucky. I make more money in a year than that white-trash security guard makes in five. I just thank the Lord I can sing. If I couldn't, I'd probably be back in Alabama swinging from a tree somewhere."

"Don't say that."

"Why not? It's true. But," he paused and flopped down next to me on the cot, "I don't want to talk about stuff like that. Dreary, dreary, dreary. So . . . you've invaded my domain at an ungodly hour of the night. I think that means we've got to talk about you."

"Oh, you already know about me."

He grinned and singsonged, "I think I mi-ight!"

"What's that supposed to mean?"

"It means, honey, that I have been to the circus and seen the clowns, and I know that when a teenaged girl don't spend all her time chattering about boys, there's probably a reason for it. And don't tell me it's because you're a good girl. I've seen you dance, and honey, you ain't no good girl."

I stared into my beer bottle as if the words I was searching for might be written inside.

"Come on, girl. You already know about me. A girl don't sit on no single cot in a dark bus with a man unless she knows she's safe with him. So what I want to know," he said, fluttering his eyelashes, "is am I safe with you, Glenda?"

I giggled. "Well, you're awful cute, but yeah, you're safe."

He grinned. "I knew it! I knew you was in the life!" He hugged a pillow against his chest. "Seeing anybody special right now?"

I saw Susan's face, but I said, "No. Not right now. How 'bout you?"

"Girl, If my voice matched my love life, I *would* be Miss Bessie Smith."

"That's too bad. You deserve somebody special. There was somebody I was with, but, uh, you remember my first day on tour when I was real quiet?"

"Uh-huh. I thought you was gonna be a queen bitch."

"Well, Susan and me had just broke up the night before. I'd come home and found her with this other girl."

"Dykeing around on you, huh?"

"I guess so. I mean, it was my fault too, a little

bit. I hadn't been treatin' her as good as I could have."

"You still love her?"

Tears welled up in my eyes. "Yeah."

"Well, maybe you ought to give her a call. See if she feels the same way about you."

"Maybe. But I'm still mad at her, too."

"Take some time, but call her."

I squeezed Octavius's hand. "Maybe I'll do that."

"I'll tell you what," he said brightly. "Why don't we make this a real slumber party? No need for either of us to sleep by our lonesome tonight, and you're safer here than you would be in bed with your own granny."

"But what if Tommy and Jeb and Les finds out about me spendin' the night out here with you?"

"Oh, I think they've got enough sense to know I ain't exactly the marrying kind. But if they don't, and they think you and I are going at it like two cats in heat . . . well, it would be kind of a kick for them to think that, wouldn't it?"

Octavius and I cuddled on that cot together not like two cats in heat, but like two kittens in the same litter curled up together for warmth and companionship.

Chapter 15

I couldn't believe it. In Dallas, about three and a half months into our tour, we were opening for Zagus Peavley. Usually in our shows, Octavius was the main attraction. I'd go on first (being the girl, I was the lowest billed — typical in those days), then Tommy, then Octavius, who'd had the most hit songs of the three of us. But Zagus Peavley was so huge it took all three of us to open for him. I knew that as a girl rockabilly singer I could never possibly be as big as Zagus, so I figured opening for him was about as high as I could get.

And I was just about as high as I could get, emotionally speaking, the day of the concert. I felt like everything in my life was just perfect except for one thing, and so of course, that one thing kept nagging at me like a hangnail you can't stop playing with even though it hurts to do it.

That one thing was Susan. I had my career, I had my music, I had my friends, but I didn't have the woman I loved. Everything would be perfect, I kept saying to myself as we headed into Dallas, if I just had Susan. Of course, everything can't be perfect all at once; life just doesn't work that way. But I didn't know that at the time.

That evening before the show, I decided to do what Octavius had told me to do months ago. I was going to call her. If nothing else, I could tell her I was opening for Zagus Peavley. She had pushed so hard for my career, she would have to be proud.

There was a pay phone outside the theater. Assuming she was still in the same place, I dialed what used to be our number. After three rings, my throat snapped shut, and I was about to hang up, but then a female voice said, "Hello?"

"Hey, Susan. Guess where I am!" I babbled. "I'm in Dallas, fixin' to open for Zagus Peavley."

There was a pause on the line, then the voice said, "Susan's out right now. Can I take a message?"

I slammed the receiver down so hard the pay phone started spitting nickels. How could she be shacked up with somebody else in our apartment? I wondered if it was that Dixie girl or some other piece of jailbait she had bowled over with her sophistication. I stormed into my dressing room, grabbed a scrap of paper, and scribbled down the words to a new song. By the time I'd finished, Jeb was knocking on my door. "You ready, Glenda?"

I slapped on some lipstick and fluffed up my hair. "Yeah," I said, clipping on my earrings, then grabbing my guitar. "I'm gonna open with a song I wrote just now. You boys follow along the best you can."

"Are you crazy?" Jeb said. "This is the biggest show we've ever played. You can't open with somethin' Les and me don't even know."

"You're smart boys. You'll catch on." I marched right past him.

As soon as the lights came up, I looked out at the biggest audience I'd ever seen, did a couple of hot licks on the guitar, then snarled into the microphone:

You're a real gone cat, you make me purr.
You know just how to stroke my fur,
But now I hear from the kittens downtown
That you've been out tom-cattin' 'round.

> *Well, the fur's gonna fly if you won't be true,*
> *Yeah, the fur's gonna fly—I'm tellin' you.*
> *I may seem tame, but beware because*
> *This little kitten's got her a set of claws.*

I hissed into the microphone, "And she knows how to use 'em. Meow!" By the second chorus, Jeb and Les were following my lead just perfect, and the kids out there were dancing in the aisles. If everybody who had ever been done wrong by a lover could let out their anger on stage in front of a thousand people, they'd feel loads better, believe me.

After that, I sang my two hit songs and the one

B side I wrote, and everybody clapped and clapped. Of course, they didn't call for an encore because they were all dying to see Zagus Peavley. But that was okay. So was I.

Tommy and Octavius played real good that night, but I was used to seeing them play good. There was nothing I was used to about Zagus Peavley's performance. To this day, I've never seen anything that could come close to it. There was something about this boy that just made him fill up whatever space he was in. No, not just fill it, overflow it. When he strutted out on that Dallas stage in his silver suit, he was the lone star in the Lone Star State.

Not to say he was a big person physically. He was slender but muscular and just about medium height. His coal black hair looked like it couldn't be forced into any style except a pompadour. Though he was supposed to be white, his skin was just a couple shades lighter than Octavius's. People said his daddy, who died when Zagus was just a baby, was a Cherokee Indian, and it could've been true, what with Zagus's high, sharp cheekbones and smoky features.

That's what he was: smoky. When I performed, I flamed with the energy of youth. Tommy shot off his guitar licks like fireworks, and Octavius exploded like an atom bomb. But Zagus's delivery smoked and bubbled like a pot on the eye of the stove that's just about to boil over. His voice was like smoke, too, warmly curling around your eardrums.

Now a lot has been said over the years about Zagus Peavley's dancing. Preachers used to rail against it, saying it was an offense to common decency. But back in Argon, when I was singing in churches, I saw people dance with that same kind of passion when they were feeling the spirit of the Lord. Zagus's swiveling hips didn't have a thing to do with sex; he was just feeling the spirit of music.

After the show was over, I was in my dressing room, getting my belongings together and drinking some whiskey Tommy had poured into a coffee cup for me. There was a soft little knock at the door. "I don't want none of what you're sellin', Octavius Richey!" I hollered. "You made me make one of the biggest mistakes of my life tonight."

A soft, husky voice said, "It ain't Octavius."

"Well, who the hell is it then?" I opened the door and found standing before me an embarrassed-acting Zagus Peavley.

I was mortified. "Oh, Mr. Peavley, I'm so sorry. I thought you —"

"Was Octavius? Yeah, I kinda figured that out." He talked in a fast mumble, running all his words together but still managing to have a Southern drawl.

"Come in if you want," I said, trying to make up for my bad manners. "I'd offer you a drink, but all I've got is this here coffee cup of whiskey."

"I'd take a sup of that if I could."

"Sure, why not? I ain't got nothin' catchin'. Nothin' I know about anyway."

"I'll take my chances." After a swallow, he said, "I just wanted to tell you I really liked your show out there tonight. I ain't seen many girls can rock that hard."

I couldn't believe the man who sang the song that changed my life was complimenting me. "Well, thank you. I didn't even know you was watchin'."

"I was watchin'. I was just hidin' out in the wings where you couldn't see me. That first song you did — whew! That was somethin'. You're a feisty little thing, ain't you?"

"I wrote that song not five minutes before I walked on stage."

"That a fact? I wondered about that, 'cause the boys in your band looked like they was about to wet their britches. Somebody make you mad before the show?"

I didn't want to talk about the phone call. If I was going to have a conversation with Zagus Peavley, it sure as hell wasn't going to be about Susan. "Maybe," I said, looking away.

"Boyfriend trouble?"

"Somethin' like that."

"Say, I got an idea," he said, "There ain't no reason for us to be sittin' here drinkin' cheap whiskey — no offense — out of a coffee cup. I got a limo waitin' for me out back with champagne chillin' in it. You like champagne, don't you?"

"Never had it."

"You'll like it. I ain't never met a girl that didn't."

The limousine was as big as a ship and was painted metallic gold. It was the most impressive and the tackiest thing I had ever seen. When we got in the backseat, where six more people could have sat comfortably, Zagus leaned up to the driver and said, "Ed, why don't you just drive us around a spell?"

The champagne was sitting in an ice bucket with two glasses, just like he'd been expecting me. When he popped the top off the bottle, I jumped like I'd heard a gunshot, and we both laughed. The champagne was the color of liquid gold, and when I swallowed it, it tickled all the way down to my belly. "Feels funny goin' down, don't it?" I said.

"Yeah," Zagus said, "fizzier than a Co-Cola."

It should've occurred to me that Zagus was out to seduce me. But I had spent the past few months drinking with guys, and it didn't mean a thing. Of course, Octavius was gay, and Tommy was married. Zagus Peavley, however, was single, gorgeous, and had the number one song on the charts, so he probably just assumed I was after him the same as every other girl on the face of the earth.

But since I didn't think of boys that way, the romantic undertones of riding in his limo and drinking champagne didn't even occur to me. As far as I was concerned, we were two rockabilly singers who respected each other's work having a friendly drink.

"You're from Kentucky, ain't you?" Zagus asked me.

"Yeah, how could you tell?"

"That accent of yours. That's a briar hopper accent if I ever heard one."

I chucked him on the arm. "Don't you be callin' me no briar hopper!"

"Hey, now, I figure a Tennessee hillbilly can call a briar hopper when he sees one." He refilled my glass. "You start singin' in church growin' up?"

"Yep. I thought it was Jesus I loved, but it was the music."

"Hey, now, don't be sayin' nothin' bad about Jesus." He reached under his shirt and pulled out a huge, diamond-studded gold cross. "Zagus Peavley can go out an' have a good time same as anybody, but there's two people he won't let you say nothin' bad about, and that's Jesus and his mama."

"You mean the virgin Mary?"

"No, I mean *my* mama. That ol' virgin Mary ain't got nothin' on Velma Peavley, except for the part about bein' a virgin. My mama raised me up by herself in a one-room shack, mendin' clothes and takin' in washin' to make ends meet."

"Hey, man, we was rich compared to you. I grew up in a *two*-room shack."

Zagus laughed. "You're a funny gal, Glenda. Say, you know the first thing I done after I made it big?"

"Uh-uh," I said, pouring us more champagne. Whiskey always made me feel heavy and tired; the champagne was making me feel like I could float away.

"I bought her a brand-new three-bedroom house and a big Cadillac."

"I got my mama a new Singer sewin' machine for her birthday this year. I wrote her a note tellin' her to make her some new dresses because I knew she'd rather fall down dead than buy a dress off the rack. A sinful waste of money, she always says."

"That sounds just like my mama."

"You know, my g — boyfriend and me used to fight about me sendin' money home to Mama."

"Well, you should just drop him then, if you ain't already. I wouldn't want to go out with a girl who didn't understand about family."

"Me neither," I said, snockered as I could be.

Zagus drained the dregs of the champagne right out of the bottle. "Cause family's important," he mumbled.

"Uh-huh."

Before I knew what was going on, he was on top of me, crushing his lips against mine and gasping, "Oh, Glenda, honey, I sure do like you."

Something stopped me from saying "stop." I was so mad at Susan that somehow in my drunk little head I thought fooling around with Zagus Peavley would teach her a lesson. Besides, I had never been with a man before, and while my body wasn't all that excited about it, my mind was kind of curious to try it. And after all, it wasn't just any old snot-nosed boy; it was Zagus Peavley. *Who knows?* I thought drunkenly. *Maybe this'll get me off women, and then no woman can ever hurt me again like Susan hurt me.*

I was lying there waiting for something to happen, and old Zagus was panting like a hound dog after a rabbit. I don't know if I should be telling you this if you're gonna put it in your book, but I feel I can testify firsthand that Zagus's gyrations on stage had nothing to do with sex. They didn't exactly make the transition from the stage to the backseat, if you know what I mean. His movements during lovemaking were somewhat uninspired, but god love him, he was probably as soused as I was, which wouldn't exactly put him at his peak performance.

The experience wasn't good or bad either one, really. I was thinking I ought to move around a little and make a few encouraging noises, but before I could even get out an "Oh, Zagus," he rolled off me and onto the floorboard and started snoring.

I fixed my clothes and pecked on the partition that separated the driver from us. The champagne tasted sickly sweet in the back of my throat, and I was queasy from rocking back and forth in the rolling car. "Uh, Ed, would you mind droppin' me off at the Winston Hotel?"

"Sure thing, miss."

I nearly tripped over Zagus getting out of the car.

"You want me to give him your phone number or anything, miss?" Ed asked.

"No, that's all right. Thank you." I knee-walked my way up to my room, fumbled with the key till I got the door open, fell on the bed, and passed out.

Chapter 16

The last place we played together was an army base in North Carolina where Tommy had lived during his short stint in the military. On the way into town, he suddenly got it into his head that we should all get a tattoo as a souvenir of our "victorious concert tour."

Octavius was having none of it. "All right, Tommy," he intoned, like a preacher gearing up for a sermon. "Let's think about this for a minute. First: No beer-bellied, gun-toting, Confederate-flag-covered-death-before-dishonor-believing North Carolina redneck tattoo artist is even gonna let me in his place of business, let alone draw pictures on my pretty black ass. Number two: Honey, look at how dark I am! You can draw with a black pen on a black piece of paper all you want to, but ain't nobody gonna be able to tell what you're drawing. Number three: Even if my skin was as white as the congregation of the Yazoo City, Mississippi First Baptist Church, there ain't no way I'm letting some greasy old redneck be poking on me with a sharp needle. Do you follow what I'm saying, Tommy?"

"Okie, if I didn't follow you, I'd either be deaf as a post or dumb as a coal bucket."

"No comment," Octavius said, looking at his long, perfectly oval fingernails.

"So how 'bout you, Glenda? You in?"

"Well, I've always kinda liked tattoos. My uncle had one when he was in the army. Of course, it was of a naked woman."

Octavius grinned. "Now there'd be a nice one for you, Glenda Fay."

"Shut up, Octavius."

The tattoo parlor was just a little hole in the wall with a sign outside that said TATTOOS WHILE U WAIT. The artist's arms were so covered in pictures you couldn't tell where one ended and the next began. He seemed a little uncomfortable having a girl in the shop. "Can I help you, honey?"

"Yeah, I want to get a tattoo."

"What of? A rose, a little heart, maybe the name of your boyfriend over there?"

"Oh lord, no." I turned to look at the designs on

the wall and saw exactly what I wanted: a tiny crescent moon with a star out from it. "Can you do this with three stars instead of one?"

"Cost you extra."

"That's not a problem." I turned to Tommy. "See — one star for you, one for Octavius, and one for me. Perfect, huh?"

"Not half bad."

I got the tattoo on the inside of my left ankle. The needle burned and stung at the same time, like a sweaty bee sting, but it really wasn't that bad. It was kind of funny, really, the way men thought putting up with this little bit of pain made them so tough. I'd take a tattoo gun over cramps any day.

Tommy got a picture of a red guitar on his upper arm, and you would've thought the tattooist was stabbing him to death. When we left, he said, "Jesus, Glenda. I don't see how you could just sit there all calm like that. Mine hurt like hell!"

After the tour was over, I turned into a hermit. I didn't have an apartment in Nashville anymore, and I was too wore out to look for one, so I checked into a hotel. For a week and a half, I did nothing but sleep, sit in the tub, read magazines, and have room service bring me my meals, which I usually left half eaten. I was too exhausted to chew, which wasn't like me. I had always had endless energy, but I figured I had finally used it up from night after night of shows, drinking, and staying up late.

After a while, though, Big Bert pestered me so much to come to the studio and record another song,

I figured I had no choice but to come out of hiding. So after a week and a half of solitude, I dragged myself out of bed, got cleaned up, and took the bus to the studio, all the while trying to convince myself that I felt like singing.

The session got off to a bad start because Big Bert thought "The Fur's Gonna Fly" was too suggestive and angry, so he wanted me to record this song a friend of his wrote called "Love My Joe" instead. If it had been about loving coffee, I might've been able to pull it off, but unfortunately, the "Joe" in the title was a boy's name. It was the first time I'd ever been asked to sing a gender-specific song, and of course, it was one that specified the wrong gender. On top of that, it was really dumb, with lyrics like, "I love my Joe/Gonna tell him so/I love my Joe/Gonna let him know/I'm just crazy about that Joe."

But I was either a real trouper or a real coward, so I finally agreed to give it my best shot. We ran through it a few times. I wasn't feeling that good, but I tried to put all the energy into it I could. Then the oddest thing happened when we started to record. The sound booth was tiny anyway, but it felt like it was getting tinier and tinier, and I felt like Floyd Collins trapped in that little space in that cave. My head started feeling like a big balloon, and my stomach was rolling and churning. My throat closed up so I couldn't sing. I threw down my guitar and gasped, "I've got to get some air." I ran out into the alley, leaned up against the building, and tried to catch my breath. Then I doubled over and vomited right there in the alley.

Now I am many things, but a puker is not one of

them. When I went back into the studio I must've looked awful because Big Bert just said, "Go home and get some more rest, Glenda. We'll pick up where we left off tomorrow."

But I didn't go home. I went to the doctor. The nurse poked me and prodded me and made me pee in a cup and bleed in a syringe. When the gray-haired old doctor finally walked in, his first words were, "Well, it's just what we suspected."

"And what's that?" I said, the hairs on the back of my neck prickling.

"You're pregnant."

I leaned over and threw up right into the trash can.

I never thought about the possibility of pregnancy when I was with Zagus. Making love with women was always worry free, and I guess I was just too drunk to think about the extra responsibilities that come with the boy-girl thing. I was having a hard time processing my situation. I had had sex with one man one time, and now I was pregnant. To make it even weirder, I was pregnant with Zagus Peavley's baby. Thousands of girls had probably claimed to be pregnant by Zagus. I actually was, and I hadn't even had that good a time getting that way!

A lot of people have asked me why I didn't get an abortion, and, honey, the honest truth is that it just didn't occur to me. Girls just didn't have choices spread out before them back then, and so it wasn't an option I was aware of. If it had been, I might've taken it.

At the time I was told, the only thing I could think of to do was run back to the studio, tell Big

Bert, and see if there was some way to salvage my career. It didn't go so good.

"You're what!" he thundered behind his closed office door.

"You heard me." I was determined to stand my ground.

"If you recall, missy, when you first walked in this door, I told you not to do anything that might be considered suggestive. Now don't you think that gettin' knocked up goes a few steps *beyond* suggestive?"

"Now, Bert —"

"This is why you can't have women in the recording industry. They pull shit like goin' out and gettin' pregnant!"

"Well, maybe it's the men in the recording industry who get 'em that way!"

"I don't even want to hear about that."

"I could hide out till the baby's born, you know, record songs but not make any appearances. That might take care of our problem."

"Miss Mooney, this is not *our* problem. This is your problem, and as of this moment, you are not Venus Records' problem!"

"What are you sayin'?"

"I'm saying that I'm releasing you from your contract. You didn't want to record that song I gave you, anyway. I guess now you don't have to."

That afternoon, I lay curled up in bed in the same position as the little creature inside me, trying to figure out my options. The only thing I knew I wasn't going to do was go back to Argon. If I went home pregnant, I'd be going home in disgrace, and

I'd have to put up with Mama praying over me and with everybody saying, "Well, she had her some big ideas, but she ended up just the same as every other gal." I wasn't going to let anybody make me ashamed.

I also decided against calling Zagus Peavley. He'd probably deny that the baby was his, and it might be even worse if he didn't deny it. What would we do — set up housekeeping in his big mansion and light the candles on the shrine to his mama in the living room every day? I wasn't going to end up married to some man just because I was pregnant. I wanted to raise this baby on my own terms, not force it to be little Velma or Zagus Peavley the second. But I also didn't want to be alone, not during my pregnancy anyway. My body had already started rebelling against me in ways I wasn't used to, and to be honest, it scared me. I wanted to be with somebody who could comfort me and tell me what I was going through was normal — that I wasn't going to die or go crazy.

Then I thought of Roy, the other prodigal child of the Mooney family, who was living with Delia in Lynnville, Georgia. Roy wouldn't judge me. I hadn't judged him when he was wild as a buck, even though I had been a Bible-toting church girl at the time. I rolled over on the bed and picked up the phone.

"Yeah?" the voice on the line grunted.

"Lord, Roy, you still ain't learned how to say hello?"

"Sissy! How you doin'? You don't sound so good."

Up until that moment, I hadn't cried. Now I was blubbering away so hard that even if I could've got some words out between sobs, he wouldn't have been able to understand them.

"Shh now, Sissy. It's all right. Nobody's dead, are they?"

"Uh-uh," I squeezed out between gasps.

"Well, if nobody's dead, I reckon whatever it is can be taken care of."

"Roy, I'm . . . gonna have . . . a baby."

"Well, Sissy, that's great! Delia just had our first'un a couple months ago, and she's just the sweetest little thing ever was."

"But it's different for me, Roy. I . . . I'm all by myself. I've been dropped from my record label. I've got nowhere to go."

"Well, that ain't true, and you know it. Tomorrow, I want you to pack up your things, hop in your car, and drive on down to Lynnville. We live at one-twenty-seven Mill Road; you write that down. We'll take care of you, Sissy."

"Now, Roy, I ain't gonna be a charity case. I intend to pay my room and board."

"We'll work that out when you get here. You and that baby just get here safe."

You and that baby. It sounded so strange.

The next morning, I took all my money out of the bank. I went to a used-car lot and bought myself a Ford. I could've bought a more luxurious car, but I knew I needed to save my money. My life wasn't about luxury anymore. I stopped at a little grocery store on the way out of town and bought me a cold Coca-Cola, which was the only thing I could imagine swallowing that wouldn't turn my stomach.

Lynnville, Georgia, didn't look much better than Argon. The textile mill, a huge, almost windowless redbrick building with chimneys sticking out from it like horns, sat square in the middle of town. There was a grocery store, a gas station, a post office, and a diner with a sign that just said EAT. The houses all looked alike — plain two-story clapboard duplexes. Since Mill Road was the main road in town, finding Roy and Delia's place wasn't a problem.

Roy swung open the front door on the right. "Hey, Sissy!" he said, draping his arm around me. "You look beat, girl. We're gonna make you rest." An ugly little pop-eyed dog shot out of the door. "That's Sam," Roy said. "Course, most of the time, we just call him 'that damn dog.' "

"I can see why." I dug into my purse and pulled out my billfold. "Now, Roy, before I even come into your house, I want to give you this." I peeled off five one-hundred-dollar bills. "Now this is a down payment on my room and board, plus all the trouble I'm gonna be."

He looked at the money in his hand. "Well, it looks like you're plannin' on bein' a whole lot of trouble." He tried to press the money back in my palm. "Sissy, I can't take your money. You'll need it when the baby comes."

"No, take it. Really. It'll make me feel better."

"All right, but this is all I'll take. I won't let you give me no more."

"Roy —"

"I'm puttin' my foot down, Sissy. Not another word about filthy lucre under my roof." He grabbed my hand and pulled me into the house.

Delia was sitting on the couch with her dress unbuttoned and the baby at her breast. "Hey, Glenda," she said, smiling. " 'Scuse me if I don't get up."

"Hey, Delia."

I must've looked down at the floor because she said, "Glenda, if you're gonna have a baby, you're gonna have to get over bein' titty-shy. The other day I flopped a tit out in front of the Baptist preacher. No need to be shy, I figure that's what they're there for."

It was weird to think about my breasts as a source of food instead of a source of pleasure. "Delia, I really appreciate this. I hope Roy didn't ask me here against your will."

"Lord, no. I'll love the company. Roy works all the time, and little Sally here's a doll, but she ain't much for conversation."

Sally dropped away from her mama's breast, sleepy and satisfied. What a tiny, fragile person. What a huge responsibility.

I wasn't much good to anybody my first couple of months at Roy and Delia's. I just lay on the couch and let Delia bring me saltines and Cokes for my nausea.

It wasn't really the nausea that was bothering me, though. It was how Mother Nature catches up with you in the end. I thought I could avoid being knocked up and wore out like all the women back in Argon, but here I was, same as everybody else. And I had thought I was so special. But nobody was special. We were just put here to grow up and make babies and die so our babies could grow up and make babies and die. So was the music God gave me just a cruel little joke to distract me from reality for a while?

I listened to the radio a lot — a rock 'n' roll station out of Atlanta that played Octavius Richey and Tommy Kain and Zagus Peavley—voices from a past that seemed very far away. Then one day, about four months into my pregnancy, the station played "Bop-a-Lot," Octavius's newest hit, and then the deejay said, "That was 'Bop-a-Lot,' played in memory of the Black Prince of rock 'n' roll, Octavius Richey. Richey and rockabilly star Tommy Kain were killed yesterday when their plane went down in rural Pennsylvania. They will be sorely missed by rock 'n' roll fans everywhere. And now here's Tommy Kain's last recording—"

"No!" I screamed, making Delia run in from the kitchen.

"What's wrong, honey? Are you in pain?"

"Tommy and Octavius . . . they're . . . they're . . . dead."

"Oh, honey, I'm so sorry."

"They were . . . my friends." I melted into a puddle of tears. Delia put her arms around me. It had been so long since a woman had held me. I cried and cried until the front of her dress was soaked through, and then suddenly the tears dried up, and somewhere inside me, the music dried up, too, until it was just a wrinkled-up little husk. Tommy and Octavius were gone, and my music was gone, too. All that was left were the little stars on my ankle, a souvenir of what we once had been. "Delia," I said, "will you teach me how to be a mama?"

The only real model of motherhood I had to go by was my own mama, so it made sense that I thought *mother*hood equaled *martyr*hood. My mama gave up being a fun-loving town girl to move to Argon and raise babies, and she never hesitated to remind us of that. And now here I was, giving up all I'd ever loved to be a mama, too.

Delia was a good teacher. She let me use little Sally as my guinea pig, which was either real generous or real stupid of her. I didn't know one end of a baby from another. I put that child's diapers on backwards and sideways and every which way but the right way, and little Sally'd just lie there on her back, wiggling her toes and looking at me like I was the craziest thing ever was. She was awful cute, with her round little face and the softest, smoothest skin, even on her little feet and elbows.

"The Lord makes babies cute," Delia said, "because if they was ugly and that much trouble, you'd just throw 'em out the window and be done with it."

Delia and me got real close. Roy left for work at six-thirty in the morning and wasn't back till after four, so the two of us kept each other company all day. We did the wash together, looked after the baby, and cooked the meals. When we got stir-crazy from being in the house all day, we'd wrap the baby up and go to the diner and drink coffee. It was one afternoon in the diner when Delia tried to get me to tell her who had got me pregnant.

"You know, I always kinda envied you when Roy'd talk about you," she said. "It seemed like you had such an excitin' life. Me, I always knowed I wasn't gonna do nothin' but get married and have babies."

"Well, maybe that's best," I said, staring into my coffee cup. "It's probably best you don't know nothin' different; that way you don't sit around wishin' for what you used to have."

"Oh, come on. You don't mean to tell me you wish you'd just stayed back in Argon like everybody else."

"I don't know, Delia. I don't even know if I wish anything anymore."

"Glenda, can I ask you somethin'?"

"I reckon."

"The daddy to your baby . . . Was he somebody famous, or just somebody you met?"

I swallowed hard, not wanting to be the pregnant lady who started crying right in the middle of the diner. "I don't want to talk about it."

Delia's eyes got real big all of a sudden. "Oh my god! It was Tommy Kain, wasn't it?"

"Delia, you're the best friend I've got right now, and I don't want to make you mad, but I really, really don't want to talk about this."

She never said another word about it. I figure she thought it was Tommy Kain, and that suited me fine. At least that way, she couldn't try to get me back together with him.

Thomas Octavius Mooney was born at nine-fifty-three P.M. October 12, 1958. The contractions had started late that morning, and by the time Roy got home from work, I was using language he had never heard a woman use in his life.

"Hey, Sissy," he said, walking into the kitchen.

About that time I felt like the whole lower half of my body had been wadded up like a piece of newspaper. I grabbed the kitchen table and doubled over, screaming, "Jesus H. Bald-Headed Christ!"

"Well, no, it's just me, Roy."

Delia took his arm. "Roy, honey, I think Glenda's about to —"

I had no patience for sweet talk. "Roy, anybody with a brain in his head would have done figured out that I'm havin' this goddamned baby right now!"

Roy looked around for a minute in a way that put me in mind of a chicken, then said, "Well, I reckon we'd better call you a doctor then."

Normally, I'd have felt funny about havin' an old man like Doc Hale hunkered down between my legs like the catcher at a baseball game, but the way I was hurting at the time, I wouldn't have noticed if the Pope himself had been staring at my private parts.

Little Tommy came out red and squawling, but healthy. I was a little worried when I first saw him because I thought he was kind of pinheaded, but Doc Hale said his head was probably just temporarily squished from being squeezed through the birth canal. "I wouldn't be sellin' him to the sideshow yet, Miss Mooney," he laughed.

I didn't know how I felt about my baby till I held him for the first time. He was all slimy and kind of addled-looking, but of course, it had been a rough night for him, too, being forced out of where it was all safe and dark and cozy into a bright room full of big, staring faces. "Hey, little Thomas Octavius," I said.

"It's an awful big name for such a little feller," Delia said.

"Yeah, but it suits him." I closed my eyes and hoped that something of Tommy and Octavius would live on in my little son. Maybe he would grow up to be a great rock 'n' roll singer. Or maybe he would just grow up to be a good man. That would be enough.

Tommy did get over being pinheaded and turned out to be so pretty his picture could have been in baby-food ads. And me, I was a baby-food factory. That boy spent so much time on my titty I felt like I ought to start mooing and slurping on a salt lick. Sometimes, when I'd sing him a lullaby, I'd get kind of weepy thinking about how much I missed my music. But I told myself I had to get over that foolishness. I was a mama now.

Music wasn't all I missed. One afternoon when Tommy and Sally were napping, I flung the bathroom door open without thinking. And there was Delia, washing her hair in the sink, wearing nothing but a princess slip. She raised up when she heard me and turned around. Her long black hair was curled up from being wet, and little dewdrops of water sparkled on the curls. The water had run down her shoulders and onto her slip, making the thin fabric cling to her curves.

I felt a wave of wanting sweep over me like I hadn't felt since I had been with Susan. Then it hit me: What the hell are you thinking, Glenda? This is your brother's wife!

Delia was towel-drying her hair. "Glenda, what's wrong? You're lookin' at me all funny."

"Nothin'. Nothin's wrong. Uh . . . excuse me."

The next morning before Roy even got up for work, I loaded little Tommy and all my belongings into the car. On the kitchen table I left a note that said,

Roy and Delia,

I have to go now but I will always remember your kindness.

Love,

Glenda

Chapter 17

I drove until I hit Atlanta, stopping once to let little Tommy have a few drags off my titty. I hadn't known Atlanta was where I was going, but when I saw the sign pointing there, I figured it was as good a place as any. It was good-sized, and I didn't want to end up in another little bitty mill town.

I drove around town till I saw a big old house with a sign that said, APARTMENT FOR RENT. It said INQUIRE IN APARTMENT #1, so I carried my sleeping baby inside and knocked on the door. An old lady in a housecoat opened it. She looked at me kind of stern, but when she saw Tommy, her face softened up. People are always nicer to you if you've got a baby with you. Unless, of course, they find out you're not married.

"Can I help you, honey?"

"Uh, yes, ma'am. I'm here to ask about the apartment for rent."

"Oh, honey, it's just a little one-bedroom apartment. You're welcome to look at it, of course, but I don't know if it'd be big enough for you and your baby and your husband."

I could tell this was her not-so-sneaky way of finding out if my baby was a bastard or, as doctors and social workers say, "illegitimate." I don't know which is worse, to call somebody a bastard or illegitimate. "Uh, I don't have a husband, ma'am," I said, trying to look as pitiful as I could. "My husband got killed in a car wreck just two months before little Tommy here was born." I waited for lightning to strike me.

"Well, bless your heart," she said. "I'm a widow, too. But I didn't lose Mr. Thomas so young." She looked at Tommy. "And such a pretty little baby, too. Just a minute, I'll get the key."

The apartment was little and plain but clean. It was partially furnished with an iron bed and chest of drawers and a table and two chairs in the kitchen. "I'll take it," I said. I handed her the first two months' rent, in cash.

That afternoon I found a used-furniture store and bought a real pretty light-blue couch and a crib for Tommy. The poor little thing had been sleeping in a bureau drawer at Roy and Delia's. I paid extra to have the furniture delivered, then went across the street to the Piggly Wiggly and bought some bread and milk and eggs and canned soup for me and some formula for Tommy. He was going to have to be a bottle baby if I was going to go out and work. And I was going to have to work. I was down to my last twenty dollars.

I drove past a Woolworth's that had HELP WANTED in the window. I figured a dime-store job was about the best I could hope for. I was a high- school dropout with no skills but music, and I was an unwed mother to boot. I straggled into that store looking dog tired and dragging a dirty-faced baby who was howling for titty. They must've felt sorry for me because they hired me on the spot.

Lord, what else is there to say about those months, those years? I worked at Woolworth's, and Mrs. Thomas took care of Tommy every weekday from nine-thirty to six-thirty until he got old enough to start school.

I stood at the candy counter measuring out bridge mix for old ladies and dime bags of jelly beans for sweaty-palmed little children. Men flirted with me a lot, telling me I was just as sweet as the candy I sold — and they all thought they were real clever for thinking of that — but I'd just hand them their bag of toffees or Starlite mints and say, "You enjoy that candy now."

I had no time for men — or for women either. The only love I let myself feel was for my son. It was motherly love that let me spend all day on my feet, being nice to all those candy buyers when I really hoped all their teeth would rot. All I let myself care about was that Tommy got the things he needed—not just food and a roof over his head but attention and love. I wanted him to have more and see more and know more than I did growing up. On my days off, I took him to the Grant Park Zoo, to the Cyclorama, or to the library. I'd read to him every day. I wanted him to love finding out about things, to be the first member of the Mooney family to graduate from high school.

If what you want to write is my life story, then there's not much for you to talk about during the years I was raising Tommy. I gave my life over to him, and I'm not saying I regret it. He turned out to be a great kid. I could bore you to death with my mama stories, from his first word to him winning the Science Fair in sixth grade, to him more than fulfilling my dream by not just graduating from high school but graduating second in his class. When I think about that kid, I'm so proud I could bust. But any mama worth her salt who's managed to raise a kid who's not a serial killer would say the same thing.

All I can say about myself during that time is what was going on with Tommy was what was going on with me. The time I spent with him I was happy. The rest of the time, when I was standing at the candy counter feeling the varicose veins pop out on my legs, I was just doing what I had to do.

And when I dreamed about a woman and woke up alone and cried into my pillow, I felt like I was doing what I had to do that way, too. Now you see all these lesbian couples raising kids, and I think it's great. But I had never heard of such a thing back then. The way I thought about it, you were either one thing or another, a gay girl or a mama. And when I got pregnant with Tommy, my body made the choice for me.

My guitar sat in its case like a body in a casket. I'd sing a kid's song to Tommy sometimes, but that was as far as my singing went, and I never turned on the radio since the day I heard Tommy Kain and Octavius Richey died. One day, I was straightening out the record bin at Woolworth's, and there, in the discount section, was a dusty old 45: "Shake It Loose" by Glenda Mooney. The girl who made that record was a complete stranger.

Chapter 18

Not only did Tommy graduate from high school, he went to college. He got accepted into this little private school in Kentucky where you don't have to pay tuition as long as you work fifteen hours a week. It just goes to show — if you're a Mooney, sooner or later, you've got to live some of your life in Kentucky.

I drove him up there. He offered to take a bus, but I wouldn't let him. I couldn't just say good-bye at some dirty bus station; I wanted to see where my baby was going to be spending the next four years of his life.

There was this one second in the car: Tommy was pushing his long hair out of his face and tucking it behind his ears like he always did, and as he did it, the light hit his cheekbones the right way, and just for a second, I saw the young Zagus Peavley.

I had told Tommy about being a rock 'n' roll singer, which he said was cool, but when he had asked me about his daddy, I just told him he was somebody I met on tour, nobody important. That was the only thing I did as a mother that I can point to and say, "That was wrong." Just because I didn't want to think about my one drunken experience with a man didn't mean Tommy didn't have a right to know who his daddy was.

Of course, I didn't think all this at that second. I just blurted out, "You looked like your daddy just then."

"My who?" His jaw dropped. Most of the time we just pretended he had come straight from me without any man's help, like those Greek gods and goddesses he used to tell me about who got born out of sea foam or something.

"Lord, son, don't just sit there with your mouth hangin' open. You don't want people at that college to think you're slow witted, do you?"

"My daddy, huh?" he said, then stared out the window like he was real interested in this field of cows.

I started crying then. I couldn't help myself. "Oh, Tommy, I was so young when I had you. Just about the age you are now. I tried to do right by you, and I think I did al

lright for the most part, but I should've told you

some things that I just didn't tell you. And I'm sorry for that."

Tommy's brown eyes squinted up behind his wire-rimmed glasses. "You said you got pregnant by somebody you met on tour. Was that not the truth?"

"Oh, it was the truth; it just wasn't enough of it. The way I said it, I could've just got myself knocked up by some little boy who'd come to see me play, but it wasn't like that. He . . . he was a musician, too." I took a deep breath and ran my finger under my eyes. "Tommy, I might as well go on and say it. Your daddy is Zagus Peavley."

Tommy did the last thing in the world I expected him to do. He busted out laughing. His face turned hot pink, and tears were streaming down his face. When he could finally speak, he gasped, "You're kidding, right?"

"No. I ain't kiddin'."

"You mean . . ." he giggled, "that guy in all those bad movies on the late show like *Hillbilly Hoedown* and *Rock 'n' Roll Ranch* is . . . my father?"

"That's about the size of it."

He beat on the dashboard, laughing. "So, even as we speak, my daddy is singing gospel songs in some casino in Las Vegas, with his eight-hundred-pound body squeezed into some god-awful sequined jump-suit?"

I started to say, "Tommy, don't talk about your daddy that way," but instead I started laughing, too, laughing so hard I had to pull off the road just like Susan had all those years ago when we got to laughing on the way to Nashville. When I could finally control myself, I said, "But he didn't used to be that way, Tommy. Back in the fifties he was the best rockabilly singer in the world. But then he went off to Hollywood and started makin' those movies, and, I don't know, it was like they just took the spirit right out of him."

"You used to date this guy?"

"Well, sort of. We, uh, we had one date, and you were the product of it."

"Mom!"

"I told you I was a wild girl, Tommy. I was real drunk that night, and I was mad at my, at somebody I'd been seein', and —"

"Who was he?"

"Who was who?"

"The guy you'd been seeing."

My hands clenched on the steering wheel. I had just talked myself into a corner. "Nobody you need to know about."

Tommy touched my arm. "It's okay. You don't have to tell me if you don't want to. Listen, I won't ask anything else about your past if you'll make me one promise."

"What's that?"

"Well, since I was born, it's been you and me. And now that I'm gonna be off at school, I want you to try to get out more and stuff. Don't let yourself get lonely, okay?"

I swallowed hard and squeezed his hand. "Okay."

The college campus looked just like it was supposed to: redbrick buildings and big, shady trees everywhere. Students stood in clumps on the sidewalks, talking. I wondered what they were talking about and if I could even understand it if I could hear them. I envied them — so bright-eyed, so energetic, with so much to learn. "You're gonna like it here, Tommy."

He smiled. "I think so, too."

Shady Grove was only about thirty minutes down the road, and after I got Tommy settled, something made me drive in that direction.

The *Barn Dance* was still there, but now it was mostly a tourist attraction. They still broadcast it over the radio, but people didn't listen to the radio like they used to. The show was in a new building — a brick theater that was nothing like a barn at all. The old barn was a T-shirt and souvenir shop now, and the old box office was a Sno-Kone stand.

The show still started at seven-thirty, and I bought a ticket. It was spooky, really. When the lights went down, a voice that didn't belong to Lonesome Joe Whitcomb called, "Paws and maws and young'uns, too/Put away your chores and kick off your shoes/Get your toes to tappin' and your mouth set to grin/Cause *Shady Grove Barn Dance* is about to begin!"

When the lights came on, the stage was decorated with the same old-timey farm tools and bales of hay, but there was a middle-aged fiddler I didn't recognize and a bunch of real young boys in the band. It was the same show with different people. There was a country comedian, an old boy wearing his overalls backward who did the same kind of cornpone humor as Miz Lucindy.

There was even a sister act, the Rugg Sisters, who wore gingham and sang "In the Pines." I kept looking at the dark-haired Rugg sister and wondering if she would like to run off and be a hell-raising rock 'n' roll singer, or was she happy where she was?

There was no way to tell. There were just two things I knew for sure. One was that *Shady Grove Barn Dance* had been frozen in time like a bug stuck in amber. The other was that the very last thing I wanted was to be frozen in time like that.

I spent that night at Vaughn and his wife Lois's little shotgun house in Morgan. Vaughn had moved from Argon when the mines closed down just like Roy had said they would. He ran a little gas station in downtown Morgan, and Lois looked after our mama, who moved in with them after the black lung finally caught up with Daddy.

Mama's mind came and went — went, mostly. She just sat in the recliner in the living room, her gray hair long and wild like a witch's, and stared at something in the distance that nobody else could see. All she said to me during my visit was, "Glenda Fay, ain't you never gonna catch you a husband?"

"What would I want with a husband, Mama?"

"Somebody to take care of you. Your daddy, he takes care of me."

Sometimes she got Vaughn confused with Daddy. It made sense; Vaughn always took after him. "Mama, I can take care of myself."

She shook her head. "Stubbornest child I ever seen," she said, then her eyes fogged over as she stared right past me.

Chapter 19

I didn't want a husband, but I did want a high-school diploma. I agreed with Tommy that it was time to do something for me, and seeing that pretty little college had got me to thinking how uneducated I was. I decided my first project now that Tommy had left home was to get myself a GED.

So one Sunday when I was out walking around and saw a bookstore, I went in. It was a new little bookstore in the same neighborhood as Woolworth's, one of several weird little businesses that had started springing up in the area, like Eardrum Records and the Horn of Plenty organic food store. The bookstore was called Athena's Owl, and there was a picture of a woman with an owl on her shoulder painted on the window.

There were about five women in the store, and all of them stared at me. And no wonder. They all looked like they'd been issued the same uniform: faded jeans, baggy shirts, flat sandals, no makeup, and short hair. Me, I was just like a bird of paradise that had walked into a flock of sparrows. I had on a white blouse with red polka dots and a matching red skirt and pumps. My hair was all poofed up from the curlers I'd slept in the night before, and I had on red lipstick and false eyelashes. I was Woolworth's and Sears and Roebuck all the way.

"May I help you, ma'am?" the clerk behind the counter asked, making me feel three hundred years old.

Another young woman who was arranging copies of a book called *Our Bodies, Ourselves* broke in before I had the chance to say anything. "Jen, you're the last person I would expect to hear using sexist language like that!"

"Like what?" the clerk asked.

"Like *ma'am.* It stands for *madam,* you know, which of course refers to a married woman. *Ma'am* is just as bad as *Mrs.* It implies that a woman can only be seen in relation to a man!"

Jen looked at her friend, then at me, trying to decide who to apologize to. She finally settled on me. "Well, I, uh —"

"That's okay, honey," I said. "When you're Southern, that ma'am just sort of slips out sometimes, don't it?"

She smiled, relieved. "I guess so."

"I was lookin' for a book on how to study for the GED. You got anything like that?"

"Yeah, I think there's a study guide over in reference. That's the last section on the left."

I found the study guide, and I also found the Athena's Owl Community Bulletin Board on the back wall. There were business cards up from massage therapists and flyers for poetry readings. One flyer in particular caught my attention:

THE ATHENA'S OWL WOMEN'S READING AND DISCUSSION CIRCLE
WEDNESDAYS AT 7 P.M.
ASK CLERK FOR MORE INFORMATION.

I walked toward the cash register.

"Did you find that study guide okay?" Jen asked.

"Yeah, and I wanted to ask you about that Women's Reading Circle."

She raised her eyebrows. "Well . . . uh . . . the first meeting is this Wednesday, and the first book we're discussing is *Rubyfruit Jungle,* but —"

"I reckon I'll just grab me a copy of that, too." The book was on a display rack in front of the counter, and I reached for a copy.

Jen was staring down at her sandals. "Um, well, sure. I mean, you're welcome to come. Any woman who wants to is welcome to come. I just don't know that you'd feel comfortable —"

"Why not? Look, if it's because I'm not educated —"

"Oh, no, no. It's nothing like that. It's just . . . here. Maybe you'd better look at the reading list."

I glanced down at the pink sheet of paper. None of the titles on it meant anything to me until I saw one that made me realize what all the fuss was about: *Lesbian/Woman.* I grinned and pointed the word *lesbian* out to Jen with a red-nailed finger. "Honey," I said, "If this here's what you was worried about, I was gettin' naked with girls before you was even a gleam in your daddy's eye."

Her mouth started out in the shape of an O but then it turned up at the corners. "In that case, I guess I'll see you Wednesday night."

"I guess you will." I flounced out of that store with my hips swinging like they hadn't in a long time. I smiled all the way home, thinking about those cute little girls with their short hair and sandals and how they were so excited about sleeping with girls they thought they'd invented it.

I stayed up all night that Sunday reading *Rubyfruit Jungle.* Sometimes I'd go back and read a part again just to make sure I'd read it right. I couldn't believe there was somebody honest enough to write about those things. I had read quite a few books while I was dating Susan, but this was the first time I'd read something where a woman talked about loving other women and being proud of it. I hadn't let myself think that way in so long it was like that book snapped me out of the coma I had been in for eighteen years.

The next day at work, I wanted to ask every person I sold candy to, "Have you ever heard of Rita Mae Brown? Have you read *Rubyfruit Jungle*?" But of course, I had better sense than to say anything. I'd get my chance on Wednesday night.

* * * * *

None of the other women in the reading group had seen their thirtieth birthday yet, and they were all dressed in those lesbian army uniforms. It wasn't like they were trying to look butch, like Susan and her old friends; they weren't trying to look masculine or feminine. They just looked kind of plain and undecorated.

I had on a yellow sundress and wedge-heeled sandals. My toenails were painted pink. Nobody could stop looking at me. I stood out like a maraschino cherry in a pile of granola.

There was this one woman I couldn't stop looking at myself, though. She was dressed like everybody else, in baggy clothes and sandals, but there was something about her that was different. Her dark eyes were hooded with heavy lids that made her look sleepy and sexy at the same time, and she had a perfect little dimple on her chin, like Robert Mitchum's, only cuter because it was on a girl. Everybody's hair was short, but hers was the shortest of all. Except for a few light brown wisps for bangs, it had been cut with clippers till it couldn't have been more than a quarter inch long. It looked soft, like down on a baby bird. I thought of touching it and felt all fluttery inside.

She felt it, too. She'd look at me, then look down at her book or inspect her fingernails like they were the most interesting thing in the world. I kept telling myself to cool it, that this woman had to be at least ten years younger than me. But it had been so long since I had looked and been looked at. It felt good.

You should've heard those girls argue, though. They picked away at that book till there was nothing left but the bones. They argued about the main character's relationships with men, about how the book depicted straight women, about Brown's criticism of butch/femme. I just sat there like I didn't have a tongue in my head. These women had been to college and knew words I wouldn't even know how to look up in a dictionary. I knew I wasn't stupid, but I sure felt ignorant.

Finally, the dimple-chinned woman looked straight at me and said, "What did you think?"

I just about jumped out of my chair. "About what?"

"About the book. I was just wondering what your opinion was."

"Oh, I loved it. Growin' up, I would've give anything to read a book where the heroine was gay and happy about it, too. It made me just want to get down on my knees and thank God you can go into a bookstore and buy somethin' like this."

The woman who had chewed Jen out for calling me ma'am said, "Don't you mean the Goddess?"

"Huh?"

"Thank the *Goddess* instead of thank *God*."

I grinned. "Well, maybe that is what I mean." The Goddess. I kind of liked that.

After the discussion was over, Dimple Chin made a beeline for me. "I hope I didn't put you on the spot," she said.

"Aah, it's good to be put on the spot every once in a while."

"Well, I wanted to make sure you got to have your say. All these women know each other. Hell, most of them have dated each other. Anyway, sometimes they won't let a new person get a word in edgewise." She held out her hand. "I'm Deb, by the way."

I took her hand and held it an extra moment. "Glenda."

"So, Glenda, what's a well-dressed lady like you doing in a bookstore full of lezzies?"

"I ended up in here accidentally one day, lookin' for a study guide for the GED."

"You wouldn't happen to need a tutor, would you? I mean, you may not, but if you need to brush up in some key areas —"

"That'd be great," I said, imagining what she could do to key areas of my body.

"How about Sunday nights around eight?"

"That'd be great."

"Here, let me write down my address. Why don't I give you my phone number, too, in case you need to get in touch with me?"

"That'd be —"

"Great?" She finished the only sentence I seemed to be capable of and smiled.

"Yeah. Great."

Deb lived in a run-down frame house that she shared with two roommates and more cats than I could keep track of. A yellow tabby was sitting on the porch when I knocked on the door, and when Deb opened it, that cat ran in, and a white long-haired cat ran out. "Hi, Glenda. Come in."

"I see you like cats."

"Yeah, the white one's Queen Christina, and the yellow one's Elizabeth Kitty Stanton."

As I walked in, a small black cat snaked around my ankles. I reached down to scratch her ears. "Now how come I get the feelin' that this one's not named Blackie?"

Deb smiled. "That's Hecate. Of course, most of the time she just gets called Hey Kitty instead."

There wasn't hardly any furniture in the living room, just big cushions to flop down on and overflowing bookshelves made out of concrete blocks and lumber. Plants were everywhere, on the floor and hanging from the ceiling, making a jungle for the cats to play in. There was a record player sitting on an orange crate on the other side of the room. I wanted to look at her records, but I was so out of touch I probably wouldn't have recognized any of them anyway.

"Make yourself comfortable, Glenda."

"Thanks." I sat down on one of the cushions on the floor, fixing my skirt so my underwear wouldn't show. I made a note to myself to wear slacks next time.

"Can I get you a cup of tea?"

"Sure, that'd be nice."

"What kind would you like?"

"I don't know. What kind you got?"

"Well, let's see . . . there's chamomile, rose hip, peppermint, lemon grass, apple-cinnamon —"

"I'll just have whatever you're havin'." The only tea I'd drunk before was Lipton.

While she was puttering around in the kitchen she said, "I hope Sunday's okay for you. It's a good night for me because my roommates aren't home, so we can study in peace."

She wanted to be alone with me. That couldn't be anything but good. "Sunday night's good for me. Of course, just about any night's good for me — My dance card ain't exactly full right now, if you know what I mean."

She came into the living room carrying a tray with two mugs and a plate of what looked like little brown bricks on it. "Really? That surprises me."

"How come?"

"I thought you'd have a busier social life." She handed me a mug and one of the little bricks. "It's a carob brownie. Tell me what you think."

It tasted like tar and wallpaper paste, but I just gnawed away at it like it was the best thing I'd ever put in my mouth. "Mmm," I said, when I'd managed to swallow a lump of it. "Actually, I've been what you might call out of circulation for a while. But I just sent my son off to college, and now I'm tryin' to get out more."

"Your son?"

"Uh-huh."

"But I thought you were a lesbian."

"Honey, we ain't sterile. I got drunk one night almost nineteen years ago, and nine months later, there was little Tommy. That was the only time I've ever been with a man."

"Wow. Do you regret it?"

"I don't regret havin' Tommy. He's a great kid."

"Wow," she said again, her dark eyes looking all serious. "Do you mind my asking you personal questions?"

"Ask away."

She asked, and I told. When I got to the part about being a rockabilly singer, she said, "Rockabilly — what's that?"

"Lord, lord," I said, shaking my head.

"What?"

"How old are you, darlin'?"

"Twenty-four."

"Uh-huh. Well, you just made me feel a hundred and twenty-four."

"I'm sorry, Glenda. But there's nothing wrong with being older. It gives you strength of character —"

"Yeah, yeah, yeah." I didn't want her to think of me as old and noble. I wanted her to think I was hot. "I'm sure you've heard rockabilly tunes before, like the old stuff Zagus Peavley did before he was a movie star."

"Tou mean 'Rock 'n' Roll Train' and stuff like that?"

"Yeah, that's rockabilly. You like it?"

"It's okay, I guess. I'm not that familiar with that much of it. I guess what little I've heard, I always thought was kind of . . . well, silly."

"You're probably right. Of course, there's nothin' wrong with a little silliness now and then to keep you from goin' crazy." Then I saw it over in the corner. I couldn't believe I'd missed it before. "Say, is that a guitar?"

She leapt up and grabbed it. "Play something for me, Glenda. Play me one of your hit songs."

When I tuned up, my fingers were shaking. I must've really been out to impress her or to run her off one, because I hadn't picked up a guitar in years.

"I'm a little rusty," I said, but then I sang "Crazy, Baby" looking right into her eyes. I remembered every chord, and I meant every word.

Finally, I managed to change the subject to her. She was the daughter of an Atlanta insurance salesman and a housewife who didn't talk to her much since they found out there weren't any wedding bells in her future. She had an English degree from Georgia State and was working at Athena's Owl and trying to decide if she wanted to go to graduate school or not. She didn't mention a girlfriend, which I took as a good sign.

"Is the guitar yours or your roommate's?" I asked her.

"It's mine."

"Good. Now you can play something for me."

"I couldn't. I'm nowhere near as good as you. I just mess around, teach myself how to play songs I like."

"Well, play me a song you like."

"Do you know 'Sisterwoman' by Hannah Christenson?"

"No, play it for me."

Her guitar work was better than she said it was, and her voice was high and clear. The song, well, it wasn't the kind of thing that hit me just right, if you know what I mean. It was real slow and sad sounding, and I think it was about lesbians, but it was hard to tell because it talked mostly about flowers and rivers and stuff like that.

"You're a pretty good little picker," I said when she'd finished.

"Hey, you know what we could do?" she said, all excited.

"No, what?" My imagination was running all over the place.

"Maybe you could give me some guitar tips in exchange for my tutoring."

"Sure," I said, although I wasn't sure I was a good enough picker anymore to be giving anybody lessons.

Deb looked at her watch. "Of course, you're probably thinking, 'What tutoring?' It's almost eleven, and we haven't gotten a damned bit of work done."

"That's okay. Maybe it was good just to get to know each other first."

"Yeah, and next time we can just jump straight into studying." She smiled and patted my hand. "Or at least spend a half hour studying for each half hour we spend gabbing."

"That sounds fair enough," I said, feeling her touch even after it was gone. "Well, I guess I ought to be goin. I've got to work in the mornin'. Thanks for the tea and the talk, though. I had a real good time."

"Me, too. Will I see you on Wednesday night for the discussion group?"

"You'll see me."

Chapter 20

Deb was driving me crazy. Every Wednesday night we sat together at the reading circle, and every Sunday night I'd go over to her house, and we'd study, practice guitar, and talk till we were blue in the face. She was smart as a whip, talking about abortion rights and vegetarianism and the myth of the vaginal orgasm. The trouble was, I wanted her to stop talking and sling me down on those floor cushions. I wanted to bring out her inner butch.

But most of the time, I was afraid the poor girl didn't even have a clue. I'd be sitting there, looking at her with absolute lust, and she'd be talking about how women had every bit as much of a right to go shirtless as men. I'd be thinking, *Let's take our shirts off now!* But something always stopped me. I don't know if it was fear of rejection or just me being an old-fashioned femme.

The morning I got my GED results, I decided it was time to take charge. After I called Tommy to tell him that his mama was a high-school graduate, I called Deb and asked her to come over and celebrate that night.

I started going through my wardrobe, looking for something to wear. My dresses all looked tacky to me, and my underwear was in truly sorry shape. After nineteen years of sleeping alone, every pair of drawers I owned was white, cotton, and torn. My brassieres had all the sex appeal of a suspension bridge. I took the bus downtown to Rich's, ready to spend more money than I had.

I bought a set of underwear: black bra, black panties, black garter belts and stockings. I tried on a scoop-necked, sleeveless black dress that came just above my knees. I looked myself up and down in the dressing room mirror. For a middle-aged mama, I didn't look half bad. I bought the dress, but I was careful to tuck the receipt into my purse. That way, if it didn't do the trick on Deb, I could always take it back.

On the way home, I picked up a bottle of champagne. I figured if a bottle of bubbly helped Zagus Peavley get a dyke into the backseat, then it couldn't hurt my chances with Deb.

By the time she knocked on the door, I had preened and primped within an inch of my life. I had on the whole garb: black dress, black undies, and a string of pearls that were really from Woolworth's.

"Wow, Glenda, you look great." She didn't look so bad herself in her white button-down shirt and faded Levi's. You could actually tell she had a body under those clothes.

"I figured now that I'm a high school graduate, I can try for a more sophisticated look. Say, do you drink champagne?"

"Not usually, but hey, we're celebrating, right?"

The cork flew out of the bottle and hit the window. We both laughed. I poured us each a tumbler full. "Sorry, I ain't got the right kind of glasses."

"Well, it's good to know there are limits to your sophistication." She took a sip and smiled. "God, Glenda, you look so pretty tonight."

I looked at her dark eyes and dimpled chin. "You always look great." I swallowed more champagne for courage. "Deb, I really appreciate everything you've done for me, not just helpin' me study, but bein' my friend. It's been really hard what with Tommy leavin' home and tryin' to get back into what my friend Octavius used to call 'the life.' " At some point during my little speech, I had let my hand come to rest on Deb's shoulder. She leaned down to kiss me, and honey, it was all over.

I fell into that kiss like it was a deep, dark well, and soon she was unzipping my dress and I was leading her back to my room and pulling her down on the bed on top of me. Her hands ran up the length of my stockings to the tops of my thighs, and soon my new dress and my new undies were thrown Goddess knows where, along with her shirt and jeans. Her mouth brushed my breasts and belly, her tongue snaking out for a quick lick here or there, her head moving down, down, down until I got self-conscious and said, "What are you doing?"

"Don't you know?"

"No, but, but . . . oh, honey, you just do whatever you want to."

Soon there was nothing but her lapping over me like water flowing over a pebble in a stream, and I was flowing, floating, flying. And then everything went black, and there was nothing in my head but music the likes of which I had never heard.

Chapter 21

That night after Deb had fallen asleep, I tiptoed into the living room, grabbed the pen and the notepad beside the phone, and wrote,

Well, Daddy worked in the coal mines,
And Mama was chained to the stove.
But me, I wanted more than that,
And so I hit the road.
My rockin' days, they went real fast,
And they were over much too soon,
But that was just one phase of the moon.

Well, life it goes in circles,
It waxes and it wanes.
One minute you're full of hope,
And the next you're a sliver of pain.
But the good times'll come round again,
And never a minute too soon,
If you just follow the phases of the moon.

Well, I raised my son the best I could,
Working for minimum pay.
But between the diapers and the teenage years,
I lost myself along the way.
But now I've found a good woman's love,
And I'm singing a happy tune.
I'm entering a new phase of the moon.

The words and music just poured out of me like they had never been gone. I crept back into the bed, spooned up against Deb, and fell into a deep, happy sleep.

I was out of bed first, making biscuits and coffee, which I took to her in bed. People who didn't grow up in the country always regard biscuits as some kind of miracle. She kept smiling, all sweet and sleepy, and saying, "I can't believe you got up and *baked* for me."

I grinned. "Honey, that's not all I did." I ran into the living room and grabbed my guitar. "I also wrote this." I sat on the edge of the bed and played my new song straight through. I was in good voice. It was different than the bubbly soda-pop voice I had as a girl. It was deep and rich, like black coffee.

When I had finished, Deb said, "You mean you wrote that last night after we —"

"Uh-huh." I leaned forward and kissed her. "I reckon you just inspired me."

"Wow, I've never been anybody's muse before."

Of course, she had to explain to me what a muse was, but after she did, I said, "Well, you can be a lot more than that."

"What do you mean?"

"I mean that I bet if you backed me up on your guitar and harmonized with me a little, the song'd sound even better."

And of course, that's how we started playing together. I already told you that as far as I'm concerned, the only things worth living for is music and love, and with Deb, I got both of them.

I started writing songs by the notebook full, and we played at bars and women's dances and private parties. For the first time, I was playing music for women to dance to with other women.

Deb and me found the cutest little apartment. It had a porch she could put her plants on, a big, sunny kitchen, and an extra bedroom for Tommy when he visited. I finally quit Woolworth's and got a job at the Horn of Plenty organic food store, measuring out scoops of lentils and couscous instead of gumdrops and chocolate-covered peanuts.

But don't you think I completely changed myself just to fit in with the women around me. I never bought the lesbian uniform, and I never got my hair cut off. Instead, I let it grow wild and long, all the way down to my behind. I didn't paint on as much of a face as I used to, but I'd still put some color on my lips and eyes when I performed. Deb always joked that we looked too butch/femme on stage together. I'd just say, "You may be the butch, honey, but you still play rhythm to my lead."

Every Sunday night we'd have all the women from Athena's Owl over to supper. They were all vegetarians, and so I'd usually cook up some beans I brought home from the Horn of Plenty. Of course, sometimes I'd sneak over to the Piggly Wiggly and buy a ham hock to cook in them. I'd feed the ham hock to the cats before the company came, and then I'd dish up some homemade corn bread with the "vegetarian" beans. Everybody always raved about how delicious they were.

Epilogue

I guess you know what happened to me, or you wouldn't be sitting here asking me these questions. Deb and me ended up getting a contract with Lavender Note Records. We've made three albums so far, and of course we play all those women's music festivals. They love us there. You know, these women are all outside, and they've been listening to nice, quiet music for the most part, and then Deb and me come on and just tear up the stage. One time when we were playing, I looked down, and all the women in the first row took their shirts off and threw them up on the stage. To be, well, over forty, and have these girls throwing their clothes at you, lord! I thought I was gonna pee in my pants right there.

And I was really surprised at all the people who remembered me from my first career. One woman came up to me at a festival and said, "I remember the first time I heard 'Crazy, Baby' on the radio, it just blew my mind. I mean, I had heard women who could sing before, but I had never heard a woman rock!"

It always kind of gets to me, too, when young girl singers tell me how I've helped pave the way for them. The gay ones, especially. That one dark-haired singer that's so popular right now came to see Deb and me play once, and afterward she came up and said, "Oh, Miss Mooney, you are just my idol. I'm a singer, too, you know. Do you have any advice to give me?"

I told her I couldn't think of nothing, that her voice was just great, but I reckoned that if I made as much money as she did, I'd sing me a *happy* song every once in a while. She got a big kick out of that.

And now there's a bunch of people trying to get me into the Rock 'n' Roll Hall of Fame. I'd be surprised if it happened, but it's real sweet of them to think of me. And you're putting me in this book you're writing. What's it called again? Yeah, *Lesbians in Rock 'n' Roll: A Herstory.*

I don't know if you'll want to put it in your book or not, but as a proud mama, I have to tell you that Tommy's a doctor now up in Lexington — a pediatrician. His wife is real smart, too — she helps run a battered women's shelter — and she's fixing to make me a grandma. They love Deb to death, say their baby's going to be real lucky to have a matching set of grandmas.

Zagus Peavley died back in 1982. He was just forty-five years old. They showed lots of films of him when he died, and I could see why Tommy had laughed when I told him who his daddy was. Zagus had turned into a big, bloated, sweaty, drug-addicted cartoon version of himself. There was none of the spark I saw in the young man I had met in Dallas all those years ago.

Bless Zagus's old heart. He let all those Hollywood and Las Vegas people suck his soul out and replace it with polyester and sequins. And in the process, he forgot what rock 'n' roll was all about: Freedom.

But me, well, there's not one thing I've done in my life I'd take back if I could, because I've got plenty of the two things in life that matter. Or maybe the three things. Music, love, and freedom.

OLD TIES by Saxon Bennett. 176 pp. Can Cleo surrender to a passionate new love? ISBN 1-56280-159-7 11.95

LOVE ON THE LINE by Laura DeHart Young. 176 pp. Will Stef win Kay's heart? ISBN 1-56280-162-7 11.95

DEVIL'S LEG CROSSING by Kaye Davis. 192 pp. 1st Maris Middleton mystery. ISBN 1-56280-158-9 11.95

COSTA BRAVA by Marta Balletbo Coll. 144 pp. Read the book, see the movie! ISBN 1-56280-153-8 11.95

MEETING MAGDALENE & OTHER STORIES by Marilyn Freeman. 144 pp. Read the book, see the movie! ISBN 1-56280-170-8 11.95

SECOND FIDDLE by Kate Calloway. 208 pp. P.I. Cassidy James' second case. ISBN 1-56280-169-6 11.95

LAUREL by Isabel Miller. 128 pp. By the author of the beloved *Patience and Sarah.* ISBN 1-56280-146-5 10.95

LOVE OR MONEY by Jackie Calhoun. 240 pp. The romance of real life. ISBN 1-56280-147-3 10.95

SMOKE AND MIRRORS by Pat Welch. 224 pp. 5th Helen Black Mystery. ISBN 1-56280-143-0 10.95

DANCING IN THE DARK edited by Barbara Grier & Christine Cassidy. 272 pp. Erotic love stories by Naiad Press authors. ISBN 1-56280-144-9 14.95

TIME AND TIME AGAIN by Catherine Ennis. 176 pp. Passionate love affair. ISBN 1-56280-145-7 10.95

PAXTON COURT by Diane Salvatore. 256 pp. Erotic and wickedly funny contemporary tale about the business of learning to live together. ISBN 1-56280-114-7 10.95

INNER CIRCLE by Claire McNab. 208 pp. 8th Carol Ashton Mystery. ISBN 1-56280-135-X 11.95

LESBIAN SEX: AN ORAL HISTORY by Susan Johnson. 240 pp. Need we say more? ISBN 1-56280-142-2 14.95

WILD THINGS by Karin Kallmaker. 240 pp. By the undisputed mistress of lesbian romance. ISBN 1-56280-139-2 11.95

THE GIRL NEXT DOOR by Mindy Kaplan. 208 pp. Just what you'd expect. ISBN 1-56280-140-6 11.95

NOW AND THEN by Penny Hayes. 240 pp. Romance on the westward journey. ISBN 1-56280-121-X 11.95

HEART ON FIRE by Diana Simmonds. 176 pp. The romantic and erotic rival of *Curious Wine.* ISBN 1-56280-152-X 11.95

DEATH AT LAVENDER BAY by Lauren Wright Douglas. 208 pp. 1st Allison O'Neil Mystery. ISBN 1-56280-085-X 11.95

YES I SAID YES I WILL by Judith McDaniel. 272 pp. Hot romance by famous author. ISBN 1-56280-138-4 11.95

FORBIDDEN FIRES by Margaret C. Anderson. Edited by Mathilda Hills. 176 pp. Famous author's "unpublished" Lesbian romance. ISBN 1-56280-123-6 21.95

SIDE TRACKS by Teresa Stores. 160 pp. Gender-bending Lesbians on the road. ISBN 1-56280-122-8 10.95

HOODED MURDER by Annette Van Dyke. 176 pp. 1st Jessie Batelle Mystery. ISBN 1-56280-134-1 10.95

WILDWOOD FLOWERS by Julia Watts. 208 pp. Hilarious and heart-warming tale of true love. ISBN 1-56280-127-9 10.95

NEVER SAY NEVER by Linda Hill. 224 pp. Rule #1: Never get involved with . . . ISBN 1-56280-126-0 10.95

THE SEARCH by Melanie McAllester. 240 pp. Exciting top cop Tenny Mendoza case. ISBN 1-56280-150-3 10.95

THE WISH LIST by Saxon Bennett. 192 pp. Romance through the years. ISBN 1-56280-125-2 10.95

FIRST IMPRESSIONS by Kate Calloway. 208 pp. P.I. Cassidy James' first case. ISBN 1-56280-133-3 10.95

OUT OF THE NIGHT by Kris Bruyer. 192 pp. Spine-tingling thriller. ISBN 1-56280-120-1 10.95

NORTHERN BLUE by Tracey Richardson. 224 pp. Police recruits Miki & Miranda — passion in the line of fire. ISBN 1-56280-118-X 10.95

LOVE'S HARVEST by Peggy J. Herring. 176 pp. by the author of *Once More With Feeling.* ISBN 1-56280-117-1 10.95

THE COLOR OF WINTER by Lisa Shapiro. 208 pp. Romantic love beyond your wildest dreams. ISBN 1-56280-116-3 10.95

FAMILY SECRETS by Laura DeHart Young. 208 pp. Enthralling romance and suspense. ISBN 1-56280-119-8 10.95

INLAND PASSAGE by Jane Rule. 288 pp. Tales exploring conventional & unconventional relationships. ISBN 0-930044-56-8 10.95

DOUBLE BLUFF by Claire McNab. 208 pp. 7th Carol Ashton Mystery. ISBN 1-56280-096-5 10.95

BAR GIRLS by Lauran Hoffman. 176 pp. See the movie, read the book! ISBN 1-56280-115-5 10.95

These are just a few of the many Naiad Press titles — we are the oldest and largest lesbian/feminist publishing company in the world. We also offer an enormous selection of lesbian video products. Please request a complete catalog. We offer personal service; we encourage and welcome direct mail orders from individuals who have limited access to bookstores carrying our publications.